THE
DARKNESS
IN LEE'S CLOSET
AND THE OTHERS WAITING THERE

To Christina,
Take Fun seriously
and make Fun of
seriousness!

—Roy

ROY SCHWARTZ

Printed by Aelurus Publishing, September 2018

Cover art and interior illustrations by Patricia Vásquez De Velasco

ISBN 13: 978-1-912775-03-3

www.aeluruspublishing.com

TO:

Arik

Guy

Nimrod

Nir

Omer

Roy

My best friends in childhood and brothers in adulthood. We may have grown old, but we shall never grow up.

Lee couldn't wait for night to arrive so she could paint again. It was the weekend, which meant she got to stay up late. This was her favorite time to paint; the night was her perfect canvas, vast and full of promise.

She spent dinner shooting eager looks at her dad. He teased her, returning a mysterious, whimsical smile. She looked to her mom for a hint, but she would betray nothing. Her big brother Ron, as usual, was oblivious, going on about something or other at school. Lee didn't pay attention. Every weekend, her dad would bring home one new item for her ever-expanding assortment of art supplies; a different tip brush, a new color paint tube, a canvas in a texture she'd never tried before. She wondered what he had gotten her this time. As soon as dinner was over she dashed to her room to wait for him. When at long last he showed up, he brought with him a whole new set of watercolors.

"I know I promised you these for your birthday, but I couldn't wait." He was almost as excited as she was. "What should we paint?"

She ran up and gave him a big hug. She thought about it, looking over all the different color options. "You!"

"Me?" He was surprised. She did, after all, paint him only a few weeks ago. "Why me? You should paint something strange and wonderful. Like your mom."

Lee laughed. He usually managed to make her laugh. She liked painting portraits, and she loved painting his most of all. His face was strong, full of shape and color with an alertness she always found inspiring.

She sat with her back to the mirror on the wall, angling the easel so he could see what she was doing and guide her. He was the one who taught her how to paint. He wasn't a professional painter—it was just a hobby—but it was a passion they both shared. And even though she was only ten and a half, she was already more talented. Or at least so he said.

She began with the outline of his head, putting down the foundation image. She had to ask him to stop making faces more than once, but as long as he held his pose and she wasn't painting his mouth, he could talk. They went late into the night discussing a million different things, mostly the big vacation they were saving up for. The family was going to Europe in the summer, to England and France and then maybe Spain or Italy. Lee had never been to a foreign country before. She was especially looking forward to seeing all the art. They were both getting so excited they were having a hard time holding still, and she ended up making a bit of a mess of his left eye. But he didn't mind. It was always about the fun of them painting together, not how the painting came out. Before long, she was done capturing him in portrait.

Lee stopped painting after her father died. He had a heart attack. Her mother found a job in a different town in a different state. When they moved, Lee didn't pack her paints.

1

Lee's new home was a small, white and red two-story house standing atop a small hill covered in apple trees. It overlooked a neighborhood of identical-looking houses arranged on a grid, as if it came out of a box. She spent most of her time alone at the house. Ron was usually out with his new friends, even on school nights, and their mom worked very long hours at her new job, managing a restaurant belonging to an old friend of hers.

She couldn't fall asleep in the new house. She tried hard. But her new room was too big: twice as wide as her old one, and twice as tall, and twice as empty. And too much moonlight seeped into it at night through its large window drapes. She could feel the light slither across the bare walls and ceiling, even with her eyes closed. One night, without really thinking about it, she decided to take her pillow and blanket and lie on the floor of her closet, which was just large enough for her to curl up in. She liked being surrounded by the total blackness. From then on, every night she would wait for her mom to look in on her, then sneak into the closet.

She had her own alarm clock, and in the mornings she would wake up a few minutes early to ruffle her bed, so it looked like it was slept in. She didn't want to make her mom worry.

For almost a month, she spent each night in the closet in the utter silence. She'd let her imagination explore the depths of the darkness around her. With every night that passed, she could swear she could see farther and farther beyond the back of the closet. She could hear distant sounds, just for a split-second, right before she would fall asleep—until one night it was as if the closet unfolded into a vast, endless darkness. Lee stared into it. The sounds that came from deep within seemed less muffled now—like people talking.

She lay there for a while, trying to make out what was being said, before it occurred to her to see if she could pass through the back of the closet. She reached out; her hand continued past where the wall should have been. She stood up, slowly put one leg forward, and, to her surprise, found solid ground. It was colder there. She took another step, becoming aware she was barefoot and wearing only pajamas. She couldn't see anything—not what she was walking on, not even her own hand when she held it right in front of her. She followed the sound of the voices for what felt like forever, until she saw a dim glow ahead of her. Tiptoeing closer and trying to be as quiet as she could, she approached the glimmering light.

She knew there were people there, but she couldn't tell yet what they looked like, only that they were all sitting around in a large room with fancy couches. The room seemed to have only one actual wall, like the set of a play, with a burning fireplace that provided light. Above the fireplace, the wall was covered in old, flowery tapestry the color of cherries, and on its mantel stood a clock with a dark wood rim carved with wild shrubbery. It was the most magnificent clock Lee had ever seen.

Something small rolled on the floor toward her and came to a stop by the edge of the fire's glow, just in front of her. She stepped into the warm light and picked it up. It was the color of ivory and weighed very little.

"Allo," came a sharp man's voice with a Spanish accent.

Lee looked up sheepishly and was about to return the pebble when she saw the man standing in front of her. Only it wasn't a man at all: It was a skeleton, smiling at her. She knew she should scream and run away—a skeleton. A smiling, talking skeleton! She wanted to, but she couldn't find her legs. All she could do was stand there, staring. He was wearing white pants, a shiny, ocean-blue short-sleeve button shirt, which clung to his ribcage, and a hat, the kind worn by men in old black and white movies only made of straw. His pants, while perfectly clean and a shade brighter than the bare bones of his feet, were zigzagged with wrinkles of all sizes, a result of having only his pelvic bones to hang from. He tipped his hat "hello," his sleeve swinging from his arm bone like a sail from a ship's mast.

"My name is Óseo Gordo. Please, call me Óseo."

He stood on one leg and bent the other across it, took the white pebble out of her hand, and snapped it into the bottom of his foot. "Yu know, there are two hundred and six bones in the human body."

"And Gordo manages to lose every single one at least once a week," a woman's voice came from Lee's right, heavy with a French accent but light as a cloud.

Lee turned her head: The woman was wearing a lilac velvet gown, with a very wide bottom that was covered in all kinds of flowers and ribbons. But where her head should have been she had a big glass jar, held in place with leather straps that ran under her arms. The jar had a small, round pillow in it that matched the dress, trimmed with golden lace and intertwining tiny peacock feathers. On it, the lady's head was placed crookedly, almost sideways, ending mid-neck. She looked a little older than Lee's mother and was very pretty, though Lee thought she wore far too much makeup.

"And that is Señora Coron," Óseo explained, "¡who only lost her head once!" He seemed very amused.

"Ze name is *Madame Couronne*," she enunciated with a magical emphasis. "And I'll have you know zat I used to be seventh in succession to ze crown of France."

"Yes, ma'am," Lee replied, trying to sound proper. She couldn't help but consider that her sanity had perhaps derailed, and all this absurdity escaped its cargo.

"Je je je je je," Óseo snickered. "Come, let me introduce yu tu the others." He reached out his boney hand to her. His smile looked gigantic without lips or gums to cover his teeth.

Though Lee generally gave herself good advice, she seldom followed it, so she took his hand. It felt lightweight and brittle. He walked her to the center of the room.

"Hello, dear," a little old lady in a green nightdress said, smiling at her from an armchair. Her voice was as warm as summertime. Her left eye was turned out a bit, but otherwise there was nothing unusual about her appearance.

"Hello, ma'am." Lee beamed back.

"What's your name, dear?"

"My name's Lee, ma'am."

"Oh, it's such a pleasure to meet such a fine, well-mannered young lady. My name is Mrs. Adocchiare." She stood up to give Lee a kiss on the cheek, but as she leaned forward, her left eye squeezed out of place with a loud, wet "*POP*," rolled over Lee's shoulder and down her back, across the floor, and under a couch. It left behind a moist trail on her pajamas that smelled like mildew.

"Oh, my!" Mrs. Adocchiare put her hand over her empty eye socket and shuffled across to the couch. "Excuse me, dear."

An old man, though not as old as Mrs. Adocchiare, got off the couch and bent down to look for the eyeball. Óseo glanced around, but was more interested in talking to Lee.

"It happens all the time. I call her Señora Cíclope," he said, giggling.

"That's not very nice," Lee protested, even though she really was a little startled, as well as a little repulsed.

"I'm afraid that Mr. Gordo here has a… shall we say, particularly unpalatable sense of humour," said the older man with a hearty British accent. He had found the eyeball and was now rubbing it clean with a monogrammed handkerchief. His round belly, which seemed to start at his knees and end at his chin, rose and heaved as he stood up. He handed the eye to Mrs. Adocchiare, who slipped it back into its socket and returned to her armchair, slightly flushed.

"I'm Percy." He offered a slight bow, making Lee feel like a princess. The top of his head was bald and shiny, and he had white hair on the back and funny fuzz on his ears. He also had bushy white eyebrows and a large handlebar mustache, which covered his mouth and curled slightly upwards. "It's a pleasure to make your acquaintance."

"Percival was on safari in Africa, and he wanted his picture taken with a rhino," Óseo said. He could barely contain himself. "And now he spends all his time calculating how much of his inheritance money his wife has spent on hats and shoes."

Lee wasn't sure what Óseo was talking about. The whole thing was very confusing, really.

"Alas," Percy stated, tucking his puffy pants into his boots, "he hath the joints of everything, but everything so out of joint. I'm afraid he's right though, darling. Tossed me around like an omelette, it did. And the Missus went on to spend all my hard-earned wealth on bloody pish-posh."

Percy sighed, shook his head, and offered Lee a seat next to him on the couch. Everybody sat down, including Madame Couronne, who sat down very slowly and gracefully, though Lee wasn't sure if it was because she was royalty or because she was afraid her jar would fall off.

"What did you pass away from, dear, if you don't mind me prying? You're so young and pretty," Mrs. Adocchiare asked with pity.

"So wise so young, it's a bloody shame." Percy nodded.

"'Passed away'?" Now, she really was starting to get scared. She wasn't dead—she couldn't be. Her heart tried to beat its way out of her chest, which she took as proof that she was still very much alive. "But I'm not dead—I just walked through the back of my closet!"

Óseo, Percy, Mrs. Adocchiare, and Madame Couronne stared at one another, looking like skeptical wax figures in the light of the fireplace.

"You mean to tell us, lass, that you got here on your own volition?" Percy's great eyebrows arched.

Lee nodded as vigorously as her neck could bear.

"Sacré bleu! Impossible," Madame Couronne declared.

"La niña está mal de la cabeza," Óseo decided.

"Shush." Mrs. Adocchiare calmed everyone down. "Lee, dear, do you think you can go back if you want to?"

She hadn't thought about it—what if she actually couldn't? What if she was now trapped in this room? She'd be all alone, and never get to see her mom or Ron again. She couldn't imagine it. She wouldn't. A shiver of cold rattled her small frame, but she didn't make a sound. It took all she had to suppress the surge of tears stinging her eyes.

She got up and walked to the edge of the light where the darkness began, with the four skittering behind her.

"If yu ask me, she is a few chocolate chips short of a cookie, sí?" Óseo scoffed.

She stood there for a minute, took a deep breath, and stepped out of the room's glow. She turned around. They were still standing in the room.

"Why won't you come out of the light?" she asked, but none of them answered. They were just looking in her direction, but they couldn't see her or hear her anymore. She stepped back in.

"¡Caramba!" Óseo gaped, and his jawbone dropped to the floor. He picked it up and snapped it back in place with a gentle click, then opened and closed his mouth a few times to make sure it worked.

"What's out zere?" Madame Couronne asked, losing her pickled pout to unbridled anticipation. "What's outside of zis room?"

"I don't know," Lee replied, as if she'd been asked to explain how gravity worked. "Just my closet." She stopped to think for a moment. "You've really never left this room?"

"We can't," Percy answered.

"How come?" she wondered.

Mrs. Adocchiare waddled over to her. "Because we don't know where to go, dear. You see, if you don't know where you're going," she explained, "you'll never get there."

Everything was finally starting to make sense—or a sort of sense, at least. She was oddly comfortable in this room, with its strange furniture and stranger fireplace and strangest occupants, walled in by darkness. And though she understood it all had to be a dream, she knew it wasn't. Her dad must have passed through there. That's why they were in her closet. That's why she could travel in and out of the darkness. So she could bring him back home.

"Have you seen my father?" she asked, wishing beyond hope. She told them his name and what he looked like: at least one of them would be able to recognize him and know where she could find him.

But they only shook their heads. Except for Madame Couronne, who pursed her lips.

"We have seen no one but each ozer since we came here." Her sigh was so full of sadness it misted the front of her jar. "Zere is just us. No one else."

Lee stared down at her feet and squirmed her naked toes about. She didn't know if she had any room left to take on their sorrow.

"How long have you been here?" she finally asked.

"We haven't the foggiest notion." Percy put on his cheerful face again, to her great relief. "To-morrow, and to-morrow, and to-morrow, creeps in this petty pace from day to day, to the last syllable of recorded time…" He paused, sneaking a glance at her to make sure his audience was properly impressed. "All we know is that we are most certainly deceased. Last I remember, I was gallavanting about the African savannah before that ill-tempered rhinoceros stripped me of my mortal coil, and I found myself in this…thing…of darkness."

She glanced around the room again. The fireplace was crackling, and sparks flew up around the clock on the mantle.

"Are you in my closet, or am I somewhere else?" she asked, even though she knew they wouldn't know.

Óseo, who stood next to Percy, pulled his hat to the back of his skull and clucked his tongue in disapproval. How he could cluck something he didn't have, or how he managed to smile at that, Lee had no idea, but since he was perfectly able to see and talk, it seemed reasonable enough.

"¿Haven't yu been listening, mi niña? We are nowhere. We did not know where tu go, so we got nowhere."

"Ach! You sound like my mum's kettle," Percy said, jumping in. "All we do know, love, is that we seem to have arrived here at the same time, regardless of when we departed."

She nodded, her thoughts racing like a herd of horses and making twice as much ruckus.

Mrs. Adocchiare sat back down in her armchair, waving at her to come over.

"Do you know what these are, dear?" She pressed her finger gently into one of Lee's dimples. Lee opened her eyes wide.

"They're the footprints of angels," Mrs. Adocchiare declared. "They sent you to us."

The idea was absolutely marvelous.

"Madam, I do say!" Percy's heavy eyebrows folded down until it looked like he had two mustaches, one below his nose and one above it. "We endure quite enough monkeyshines from this fellow of infinite jest." He twitched his head at Óseo, who on his part flashed a broad grin at Lee and shrugged his shoulders, causing his right collarbone to fall down his shirt, clinking and clanking its way out his sagging pant leg. She almost managed to stifle a giggle. Percy, without turning around, just closed his eyes halfway and took a long, deep breath. "This devout drivel is uncalled for. Really, a woman of your years, speaking of angels. Such humbug. Humph." His mustache—the real one—wiggle-waggled like a small, jittery dog shaking off its wet fur.

"Oh, don't you listen to that stuffy old walrus, Lee, dear." Mrs. Adocchiare took her hand within both of hers. "All he ever believed in was collecting money and trophies—collecting and collecting and collecting until *he* was collected." She telegraphed a smile of satisfaction across the room to Percy, who didn't look amused, but did look a bit like a walrus.

"Yes, yes, indeed. And while our saintly Mrs. Adocchiare is full to the brim with the holy spirits and what have you, the rest of us have a high moral obligation to be rational."

Madame Couronne put her hands to the side of her jar. "Mon dieu! You two are giving me a migraine again."

Lee could tell it was a friendly bickering, more of a show put on for her benefit.

Eager to change the subject, Óseo made use of the short moment of silence to introduce a topic of his own into the conversation. "Tell me, chica," he said, winking at Lee, "¿What du yu du?"

She tilted her head in question.

"¿Outside of here—what du yu du?"

"I… go to school." She wasn't quite sure if that's what he meant. He seemed unsatisfied.

"¿Du yu like yur school?"

"It's okay, I guess."

"Bueno… ¿what du yu du for fun then, eh?"

"I don't know…" she mumbled, still unsure.

"¿'*Don't know*'?" His head rattled to the side. "I du not understand. ¿How can yu not know?" He paused to think, looking like a picture hung off its center.

"Yu must have a passion that sets yur blood on fire. No wonder yu have such a sad look, niña."

"But I'm not sad," she protested. If anything, she was enjoying herself more than she had in quite a while.

"I didn't say yu were sad; I said yu have a sad *look*," he clarified. "It's in yur eyes."

Mrs. Adocchiare brushed her fingers through Lee's hair. They felt like chubby little sticks of sponge rolling across her scalp.

"The poor dear looks like a poor deer," she offered compassionately, lingering on "deer" for distinction. "She misses her father, don't you, sweetie?" Mrs. Adocchiare was about to say something consoling when Percy interjected. "What's all this, then? Young lady, I'll have you know that throughout my many years of travel, I have developed a rather keen eye for character, and you, my dear, are neither dull nor idle." His voice became gentler as he continued, "Surely, there is *something* that uplifts your spirit?"

She hesitated for a dozen long heartbeats. "Um… I used to paint, a lot," she admitted, not sure she cared to. "All the time…"

"Jolly good." Percy was pleased to no end.

"But I don't anymore, really," she quickly added.

"Well, then yu should start painting again," Óseo said.

She hung her head, following her shadow dance across the dark wooden floor to the skittering rhythm of the fireplace flames.

"I… I don't know."

Percy lowered himself into the couch, leaning against his knees with a drawn-out groan, and looked back at her, now at the same height.

"Whether you believe you can do a thing or not, dear, you are right." He smiled in an understanding way.

"Mi Bonita, it is very simple," Óseo continued enthusiastically. "To begin something, yu begin at the beginning. And if it is not the beginning, yu go back and begin again."

She couldn't help but giggle, then broke into outright laughter. Soon, they all joined in. Even Madame Couronne, who did her best to seem uninterested, let escape a pearl of titters, filling the room with her voice, sweet and clear, like the scent of flowers filling a greenhouse.

Lee wanted to ask them a million more questions, but she was starting to get sleepy, and her eyelids were becoming heavy.

"Can I come visit you tomorrow night?" she asked.

All four seemed more than pleased with the idea.

"Claro niña, yu can come whenever yu want—we cannot divide day and night here," Óseo answered.

"I shall say good night till it be morrow, then." Percy stood up and bowed again, and with that, she waved them goodbye and returned to her closet.

The next day at school was excruciating. Nightfall could not come fast enough for Lee to go back and visit her new friends. The only friends she'd made since she moved. The weird adventure from the night before replayed itself in her head: in her first period math class, Mrs. Faloola scolded her for daydreaming. But in second period biology, Mr. Lehrer introduced the class to a plastic skeleton, and Lee knew the answer to how many bones it had—two hundred and six, of course—so she got to name it Óseo.

Last period stretched like gum. When the bell finally rang, she dashed out the door before she could be swallowed up in a squealing wave of schoolbags and pom-poms.

Lee had spotted before an old arts and crafts store a few blocks down from the school, but had always avoided it. She ran inside, coming out having parted ways with her entire allowance savings but carrying a side bag filled with brushes, a few small canvases, a collapsible easel, and a new set of watercolors—the same one her father had bought her.

As nightfall approached she could barely contain herself. Her mom made it home in time for dinner, bringing food from work. She even brought chocolate cheesecake for Lee and strawberry shortcake for Ron, their favorites. She was trying so very hard, Lee knew. She loved her mom, but she missed her, even when she was home. She missed the family they used to be.

Finally, her mom came to tuck her in and say goodnight. After waiting a little, Lee dove into the closet. Only this time she took with her the new bag of art supplies and easel, as well as a flashlight, and *The Wonderful Wizard of Oz*, which was a reading assignment for school. Since the passage through the darkness had been quite cold before, she wore her

bootie slippers and flannel pajamas, a shirt and pants with pockets in a white and blue pattern.

She read for a long time, almost five chapters, but she could still make out the wall at the back of the closet. She thought that maybe it needed to be completely dark for it to open, so she put the book down and turned off the flashlight. She sat in the dark and listened for the voices in complete silence, barely allowing herself to breath. Soon, she started to become drowsy. She yawned, and only when the hum of her own yawn died down, she could hear the faint murmurs of the others, and the darkness of the closet opened again into the cold void.

She found Óseo stoking the fireplace, while Percy was holding up the end of a couch for Mrs. Adocchiare to sweep under. Madame Couronne's body was sitting on another couch in front of the table, where her head rested upright on its pillow outside the jar. She was fixing her makeup.

"Hello," Lee called out.

"Hallo there," Percy answered cheerfully.

"¡Hola!" Óseo yelled from over the fireplace.

Madame Couronne paused to nod at her, then went back to her makeup.

"How've you been, dear?" asked Mrs. Adocchiare.

"I've been waiting all day to come back." Lee smiled.

"Oh," Mrs. Adocchiare said, seeming puzzled. "Dear me, has tomorrow come already?"

Lee nodded. "Mm-hmm."

"Je je je je je." Óseo was prodding the firewood like a sculptor putting the finishing touches on his masterpiece. "Tomorrow of yesterday is today of today, sí?"

"Well, darling," Percy said, winking with both his eyes at her. "Your visit positively put us in high spirits."

"Really?" She was very pleased to hear it.

"¡Pues claro que sí!" Óseo said as he stood up and brushed the soot off his hands. One of his fingers came off and fell into the fireplace, and he dashed to roll it out with his poker before it got burnt.

Lee skipped over to him. "We started to learn about the skeleton in school today."

"¡Ja!" Óseo sneered. "¿And what did they teach yu?"

"I knew how many bones it has," she declared proudly. "Two hundred and six. And we learned about the spine—it has thirty-three vertebras."

"Sí," Óseo challenged, "¿but can yu name them?"

She shook her head.

"The human spinal column consists of five sections." Óseo held up the finger he dropped, wiggling it in the air. "Seven cervical vertebrae, twelve thoracical, five lumbaric, four sacral, and four coccygeal. ¿Sí?"

She nodded, pretending to understand.

"Now listen here, chap!" Percy's hair frizzled around the shiny top of his head. "The girl did not come here all the way from her wardrobe just so she could listen to your poppycock."

She could tell Óseo was rolling his eyes.

"What do you think, madam?" Percy peeked under the couch he was holding up, where Mrs. Adocchiare was still sweeping.

24

"Oh, I usually don't know what I think until I see what I say," she said, giggling. She stood up. "It's hard work, to be thinking all the time, you know," she teased Lee.

"Which is probably ze reason why so few engage in it," Madame Couronne contributed her own punchline. Óseo seemed impressed, and her head gave him a playful wink as she put it back in the jar.

"Mind you, nobody likes a blatherskite. And you, sir, are a *blatherskite*." Percy crinkled his great white eyebrows at Óseo.

"¿Qué quiere decri 'blatherskite'?" Óseo finished reattaching his finger, and seemed genuinely interested.

"Blatherskite, sir, is a long-winded know-it-all, who takes every opportunity to interject their claptrap into any conversation, unmindful of social decorum."

Everyone, including Lee, stared amused at Percy, until the irony fell on him.

"Oh, fiddlesticks!" He plunged into the couch with crossed arms, releasing a puff of dust around him.

Mrs. Adocchiare, by this point, had already moved on to the mantel, and was hard at work dusting the clock with the elegant carvings. Without pausing she turned to Lee. "Lee, dear, how's your painting coming along? I'm very much looking forward to seeing your newest creations," she inquired.

"I was only here yesterday," Lee pointed out, "so I didn't paint anything yet—"

"Oh, right you are, dear. Silly me." She chuckled.

"But I brought paints and supplies today. Want to see?"

"Oh, how exciting." Mrs. Adocchiare seemed thrilled.

Óseo seemed just as keen, chattering something in Spanish, while Percy, still sulking, limited himself to a squiggly line of a smile. Madame Couronne skillfully expressed with one look that she was rather indifferent, but since she had nothing better to do, she might as well encourage Lee.

Lee beamed every color of the rainbow in delight. She reached for her bag and took out the small heap of canvases and paints and brushes, parading them to the center of the room, the easel hanging off her shoulder. All seemed very impressed.

"Muy bien, niña." Óseo held up his bony thumb in approval. "Yu paint something for us now, sí?"

"Smashing!" Percy seconded the idea.

She tried to think of something impressive to paint for them, but nothing came to mind. She was starting to become frustrated.

"Sweetie, would you paint me something if I asked you to?" Mrs. Adocchiare caught on.

She nodded, happy.

"When I was about your age, I had a pet bird. Could you paint that for me? A bird with beautiful colors?" The awakened memory clearly warmed up the kind old lady.

"Sure." Lee liked the idea right away, especially since she'd painted birds before.

When she had finished setting up and mixing the paints on her palette, she made the first brushstroke. She wasn't quite sure how to begin. It had been a while since she last painted, together with her father. But the instant the brush touched the canvas, all her anxiousness dissolved. It was as if she had been holding her breath all this time and finally took her first lungful of air.

The bird came easily. It was vivid in her mind as though she had seen it herself. She used a royal blue for the bird's body and gave it a crown of rich crimson, along with some bright red streaks across the tail. For the wing feathers, she decided on lush orange and yellow, and she left a patch of white across its chest. Altogether, she was very pleased with the outcome.

She hadn't noticed before that moment, but the clock on the mantle, which had been completely still, began ticking, and its hands moved as she started to paint. She looked around, but the four seemed oblivious to the sound.

Something small and very quick flew in from the darkness and fluttered around the room chirping loudly—a little bird. It startled Percy, who jolted back in his couch and discharged an expression of complete and total wonder. Madame Couronne convulsed as the bird whizzed by, almost tipping over her jar. Óseo, who was kneeling by the fireplace, shot up, transfixed. Mrs. Adocchiare looked over in astonishment at Lee, who herself stood mesmerized.

The bird circled the room a few times, filling it with song, until it finally settled atop the back of one of the couches. It was blue with a white chest, a red crown, and orange and yellow wings. The bird Lee had painted.

"Heavens!" Mrs. Adocchiare was the first to release an exclamation.

"Mon dieu," Madame Couronne whispered in awe, squinting her eyes at the feathered creature.

Percy and Óseo glanced at the bird, then at each other, then at Lee. Percy leaned in toward her in hopes she would know what to make of it.

"I… I…" She had no better idea than they did.

The bird seemed oblivious to the commotion it had caused and was inspecting the room from its perch atop the couch.

"Lee, dearie," Mrs. Adocchiare said, "quick—paint another one!"

The others unglued themselves from place, gesturing encouragingly.

"Sí, sí, paint again," Óseo said.

She wasn't quite sure what Mrs. Adocchiare had in mind, so she set about to paint a new bird. She gave this one a green jacket of feathers, a bright blue belly, and speckled its wings with majestic purple and lily white. This time she listened for the ticking of the mantelpiece clock. As before, she could hear it accompanying her while she painted.

When she was done, she peered out into the darkness, waiting for the bird to emerge. Percy, Óseo, Mrs. Adocchiare, and Madame Couronne held their breath in anticipation.

Nothing.

She craned her neck around. Still nothing.

A moment came and went.

She walked past them toward the end of the room, standing at the outer rim of the firelight. She stared into the void as intensely as she could. She stared even harder.

A small, green bird zipped right by her, disheveling her hair. It joined the blue bird in flight around the room, chirruping as loudly as their tiny lungs could possibly allow. They crisscrossed the room in a trajectory of noise and color like ribbons twirling around each other in the wind, around and about and eventually out of the room, back into the darkness. And just like that, everything went quiet again.

"Hurrah!" Percy cheered wildly. He shot out of his couch like a cannonball, his excitement infecting the others.

"How delightful," Mrs. Adocchiare joined him in a little dance around the table. Óseo joined in on the merriment and even Madame Couronne smiled, offering a sincere, "Amazing."

Wild hope lit up in Lee. This endless darkness she had wandered into gave form to the two birds she'd painted. Here, she had the power to bring alive the creations of her mind. Or the desperate desires of her heart.

"This is how. This is how I'll bring my dad back!" She jumped up and down. "I can paint him, and he'll come here. And then I can take him home." She couldn't stop shaking with excitement. She imagined her mom's and Ron's faces when she and her dad walked into the house together. They'd be a family again.

"Jolly good." Percy resumed the festivity with vigor, sweeping along even Madame Couronne, who gave a short burst of light clapping. Mrs. Adocchiare was so excited that she teared with joy, but she had to stop because the tears made her left eyeball roll in place, which made her dizzy.

"Je je je. Señora Cíclope is very happy for yu." Óseo smiled as he made his way to Lee. He knelt down in front of her, placing his bony hand on her shoulder.

"I couldn't be happier for yu too, niña. We all are." He had the same look of promise Lee had—unreasonable hope, rekindled.

"¿Du yu think, after yu find yur father, yu can help us out of here? We have been stuck in this place for a very long time."

She nodded. If painting could invite things into the room, it stood to reason that painting could also free those inside it.

"You want to come back home with us?" she asked.

Percy laughed. "No, dear girl. We are all dead beyond help, I'm afraid. What we seek is not to return to lives long past, but to move on to whatever awaits us in the great hereafter."

Lee's task was clear. She placed a new canvas on the easel and arranged new paints on her palette. She was so jittery she couldn't keep her hands from shaking, but the painting had to be absolutely perfect this time, so she stopped, closed her eyes, and took a slow, deep breath, all the way down to calm her churning stomach. She conjured up a clear memory of her father.

When she could see his face clearly in front of her—his eyes, his smile, the way she remembered him from the last time she saw him—she opened her eyes and started tracing it on the canvas. And soon enough, he was looking back at her from the painted sheet.

She flopped down on the couch between Mrs. Adocchiare and Percy. The five sat in silence, except for the ticking clock.

The minutes tiptoed by, the hands of the clock conducting their rhythm:

Tick.

Tock.

Tick.

Tock.

Tick.

Tock.

Tick.

Tock.

They waited for a long time, much longer than it had taken the birds to appear, but there was no sign of her father. She couldn't sit still any longer. She ran to the darkness, looking to see if there was something there—any indication at all—but there was nothing. She ran to the other side of the room; perhaps he was coming through that way. Still nothing. She ran from one end to the other, pacing across every which way a hundred times over. He wasn't coming. Her eyes spilled over with tears, tears that had been building up behind them for months. She began to sob.

"You dear thing." Mrs. Adocchiare's face filled with pity, as did Percy's and Madame Couronne's.

Óseo, for the first time, had nothing to say. He gave her a hug, as strong and as warm as a skeleton can. Her tears stained his silken blue shirt.

A piece of log crackled apart in the fire, instigating a shower of sparks up into the room. It startled Mrs. Adocchiare, who was sitting closest.

"Look. *Look!*" Madame Couronne cried abruptly, waving her finger at the darkness.

Lee rubbed her eyes on her sleeve and looked to where Madame Couronne pointed. There was something different about the darkness. She focused through the veil of tears; the darkness was twinkling. All around the room, on all sides and above, there were tiny glimmering lights. Stars. It was the night's sky.

"Estrellas…" Óseo murmured in disbelief.

Percy, Mrs. Adocchiare, and Madame Couronne stood up, fixated on the spectacle surrounding them. They didn't blink once. They didn't dare to.

Lee turned around in place, examining the studded sky. She felt wind blowing on her face. She walked toward the edge of the room and reached out. Her hand was not swallowed in a wall of darkness. It just hung in the open night air.

"By Jove…" Percy reached for his robust mustache and rubbed it. "Strange goings-on, indeed."

"Aleluya," Óseo said, once his astonishment had sufficiently ebbed.

Mrs. Adocchiare exchanged eager smiles with Lee, but Madame Couronne was still astounded. She looked out her jar with an expression almost of doubt, like she was afraid of committing to what she was seeing.

"Zis… chamber," she asked cautiously, "we can now… leave here?"

"Yes," Lee replied with confidence, realizing why the room had opened out. "My dad's somewhere out there." She pointed to the starry distance. "I have to go find my dad. I'm going to go find him and bring him back." Her painting may not have brought him to her, but it showed her the way to him. And she was brave enough to follow, she decided.

"The girl is right; I'd wager my finest waistcoat on it." Percy said. "Come on then—we shall accompany her on this expedition."

She was tremendously relieved to hear this. She was more than a little afraid of continuing on her own.

Madame Couronne pursed her ruby red lips. "I do not zink, zat after all zis time in zis huis-clos room, we sh—"

"Balderdash," Percy cut her short. "Every questing young princess should have her band of knights in accompaniment." He winked at Lee. "Forsooth—my spirit craves adventure!" He grabbed a poker by the fireplace and brandished it like a sword. It made Lee laugh.

"Mon dieu! It's like trying to carry on a conversation wiz a cantaloupe," Madame Couronne cried out, waving outstretched fingers.

Mrs. Adocchiare turned to Óseo, who was leaning against the flower tapestry wall with hands in pockets, for his opinion.

"I am an esqueleto. I have no other marshal but fortune tu arrange my bits," he said lightheartedly.

"And I du not know what lies ahead. So I say we go with Lee."

Percy was pleased, but Madame Couronne was still hesitant, and the four broke into yet another quarrel. It was less of an argument and more of a ritual, Lee knew, practiced for so long it had become as comfortable as a worn-out old sweatshirt.

"Sigh. Very well zen," Madame Couronne said, eventually won over, and the five prepared to embark on their journey. Lee packed her art supplies into her bag and slung it across, leaving behind the easel. Her heart pounded a thunderstorm of both thrill and dread; for all her courage, a cloud of doubt loomed heavily above her. But she recruited her strongest resolution. Her mission was simply too important to let herself be intimidated.

"Well, well, let's get on with it," Percy encouraged her, and she skipped out of the room and into the night. He followed with a spirited "Tally ho!" Mrs. Adocchiare, having hastily primmed her cotton candy-like hair, stepped closely behind. Madame Couronne hesitated for a long moment at the end of the room, but eventually picked up her ample gown and pouted her way out. Óseo held on to his straw hat and whistled by.

III

They had not gotten far when day broke around them. The night was fading now into dark pinks and dull reds and lazy oranges. There was no sun that Lee could detect anywhere in the sky, but it was nevertheless busy burning away the morning haze, slowly revealing a vast expanse of dark green flatland before them. The air smelled like grass after the rain.

There were all sorts of odd and extraordinary things there Lee had never seen before. The clouds looked like giant fingerprints smudged against the bright sky. Here and there naked, twisted trees interrupted the otherwise level view, their whorling limbs reaching out like arms, as if to clutch at passersby. There were also strange flowers about with red petals that turned black toward their edges, forming collars for little saw-toothed flaps, like traps. Crawling around them were giant centipedes, each almost as long and as wide as Lee's leg, burrowing in and out of the ground.

"We should remain wizin easy distance of ze room," Madame Couronne suggested, the gold embroidery of her pillow glistening in the sun. But the others continued on, oblivious to her warning. They were far more engrossed in the surrounding scenery—they hadn't seen daylight in untold ages.

Conversation was kept to a minimum as everyone was preoccupied with their own thoughts. They walked on for a long time, even though the landscape provided no indication of how much time had passed. It offered only more of the same. But Lee knew they had covered quite a distance by making note of the different shapes of the trees and clouds, as well as by how tired she was getting.

Sooner or later—it was hard to say for sure—they came across something new; not far from them was a silhouette of an occupied hammock hanging high between two trees, in the shade provided by their tangled branches.

"Be careful, Lee, dear. It could be dangerous," Mrs. Adocchiare said.

Lee wasn't careful. She ran up to the figure sleeping in the hammock.

"Halloo! Halloo there I say," Percy called ahead of her. He startled the person, who catapulted onto the ground just as Lee reached him. He was very short, about her height, with a stocky, muscular build.

"Hello," she said.

The man nodded, having not completely awakened yet. She then noticed that the dome of his head was missing; it ended halfway through his forehead, and inside it was a bird's nest with three tweeting chicks.

She was startled, but only for a moment. She had a feeling it wouldn't be the last strange thing she'd see.

"I say, good fellow," Percy said, having arrived, excited to meet another new person.

"Who're you?" the little man demanded in a gruff voice. Clearly, he was not accustomed to company, or the manners that come with it.

"Sir Percival Alistair Wordsworth, at your service." Percy squared off his shoulders and gestured a short bow. "And the young lady here is Lee."

"Brevis," the man offered in response.

"Humph. Well, what's in a name, eh?" Percy tried to goad Brevis into saying more. It appeared to work.

"I have a splitting headache," he moaned, rubbing across the folds of his forehead. "But I can't tell if it's from the constant *chirp-chirp-chirp* I have to deal with all day long or the hole I have in my head."

"How did yu get a head full of birds?" Óseo asked, just as he and the ladies caught up.

"I think their mother built the nest one day while I was sleeping. I woke up and hadn't suspected a thing, and by the time the chicks popped out of my head, I didn't know where the mother had gone. So now I'm responsible for them."

He pulled out of his pocket a little brown pouch and took a small amount of grains and seeds. He chewed on them until they were crushed, then reached up and tenderly sprinkled the soggy crumbles into the chicks' squeaking beaks. Lee found it a little disgusting but also very sweet.

"So what brings a diverse group of dead folks such as yourselves to these forgotten parts?" Brevis inquired.

"Oh, we're not all dead—" Lee started.

"You're all dead." Brevis stated with confidence.

"But I don't want to be dead," Lee remarked. It seemed unfair she should be judged by the company she kept.

"You can't help that," Brevis said. "We're all dead here. I'm dead. You're dead."

"How do you know I'm dead?" Lee asked.

"You must be," he said, "or you wouldn't have come here."

"But I'm not dead at all!" Lee objected. "I'm very alive. And I'm here because I'm looking for my dad."

"Well, it's extremely rude to depart from the company of the living before you die. It's very offensive." Brevis seemed to take the matter rather personally.

"I assure you, kind sir, we had no intention of giving offense," Percy hurried to say.

Lee nodded earnestly. Brevis seemed satisfied.

"Where are we?" she asked.

"Why, we're right here of course," Brevis said. "What a silly question. Are you trying to be sassy now?"

"No. I promise," she said. "I was just wondering what's the name of this place?"

"Well, why didn't you say so?" Brevis threw his brawny arms up. "I believe it's called the Middle of Nowhere." He stopped to think for a moment. "It's not quite any place really. But I'm pretty sure we're at the heart of it."

"Why is it called it that?" Mrs. Adocchiare asked. Lee thought her shyness had kept her out of the conversation, but it seemed that her curiosity won over.

"Have you never been lost?" Brevis retorted. "Well, it's exactly the same. If you're lost to the world, you find yourself in the Middle of Nowhere. Then you move on to Elsewhere. It's pretty obvious, really."

"I see," Mrs. Adocchiare said, even though it was quite clear she didn't.

Brevis put up his head and looked around to see what she was talking about. "What? What is it?"

Mrs. Adocchiare tried to clear the confusion. "Oh, nothing—"

"Then how can you see? You either see something or you don't see anything at all. If you see nothing, then what are you seeing?"

The three birds in Brevis's hollow head had not stopped *chirp-chirp-chirp*-ing, and Lee was growing restless. She tugged on Óseo's sleeve; she wanted to leave, to find her father as soon as possible. Óseo tilted his head to hint at Percy.

"Hmm, yes. Tell me, old chap," Percy addressed Brevis, "might you do us a favour and direct us to where we may locate the girl's father?"

Brevis mulled it over and pointed at the horizon to their left. It looked no different to Lee than anything else around.

"I wouldn't know. But there's a small village about a day's march away in that direction. They might know."

"Jolly good. Kind thanks, sir." Percy tapped Lee on the back. "Come along, now."

She waved at Brevis, who waved back and jumped up into his hammock. Madame Couronne said "merci beaucoup," her only contribution to the conversation, and the five of them took off.

IV

They stopped a couple of times along the way for rest, but only because Percy, Madame Couronne, and Mrs. Adocchiare were winded, which, Lee learned, the dead can be. She was anxious. She wanted to reach the village before nightfall. The sky was starting to darken, and the bright blues and yellows slowly were being replaced by violets and crimsons. She didn't like the idea of stepping among the giant centipedes in the dark.

At her urging the five picked up their pace, with her spearheading the way and Óseo bringing up the rear to make sure Madame Couronne and Mrs. Adocchiare kept up. But ultimately, they found themselves walking under the stars, which to her surprise provided more than enough light, casting a soft, bluish glow.

The skies around them seemed to have awakened to the night, filling up with odd squawks and shrieks and eerie coos, carried by the breezes as they swept across the grassy plain.

Something large crept across the ground in front of her. She stopped dead in her tracks. The leaves of grass parted as it moved toward her. She braced herself. It came slinking out and she yelped, recoiling. A massive, shiny black-green beetle crawled past. Its body was severed into two halves, with its hind part scurrying to catch up to its front.

"Je je je je. It brought yur heart tu yur mouth, sí?" Óseo snickered.

She was disappointed in herself for scaring so easily. She knew she needed to be braver if she intended to find her father.

The land gradually became uneven and hilly as they continued on. Not far ahead, Lee could make out the shape of a house, sitting on a ridge. They ran up to the small cabin and knocked on the door. No one answered.

"Look," Mrs. Adocchiare whispered.

On the other side of the house, at the bottom of the hill, was a small campsite, with the remains of a bonfire at its center. The firewood was still glowing red, and Lee could feel its inviting warmth. A large log was set in front of it, and on it sat a plump kid, roughly Lee's age but possibly a little older. He wore loose-fitting shorts made of stained dark leather that continued as suspenders around his shoulders. The pants gathered just above his doughy knees, with white tube socks ending just below. His face was squeezed between fleshy cheeks and rolling chins like a kitten fallen between the pillows of a sofa. He gave Lee and the others a slow smile.

"Hi," Lee said.

"Guten abend," the boy replied, sluggishly.

"I'm Lee. These are my friends." The four gestured hello.

"Mein name ist Heinrich Rundlich," he said in the same slow pace.

"Do you live here by yourself?" Lee said.

"Ya," he replied. He remained seated on the log near the burning coals, staring stupidly into the sky. He was looking up into the sky all the time he was speaking, and this Lee thought impolite, though she wasn't quite sure what to make of him. His eyes were half closed like shutters and his mouth hung open like a hinged door. Had his head been a house, it was clear no one would have been home.

"We heard there's a village around here. Do you know where it is?" asked Lee. "Ya." The boy nodded.

"Wonderful," Madame Couronne said sarcastically.

"Can you show us?" Lee said.

"Ya." He hopped off the bench and signaled her and the others to follow. On their way past the cabin, he went inside and returned holding on to a large silver balloon shaped like a fish. It floated above him in the air and guided their way by the direction it was facing. Its eyes looked like the boy's.

The six of them followed the balloon, as if they were taking a nightly stroll along the countryside. It was frustrating. Lee wanted to get to the village as quickly as possible, so she could find her dad and get back home to her mom and Ron, but they could only go as fast as the little pattering of the boy's feet.

"Dort drüben." He eventually pointed over at a collection of houses, sitting in a crevice formed by the lumps and hills. He smiled at them and lollopped back into the night.

The village seemed like a county fair built in a large hole in the ground. It consisted of no more than twenty houses, all made of clay and roofed with straw. Strings of hanging lights were strewn between the surrounding hilltops, illuminating the place in uneven bright and dark spots. Lee could hear festive sounds coming from its center courtyard, like a waterfall hitting the rocks at its base.

"¡Ooh, es una fiesta!" Óseo hooted, grabbing Lee by the hand and scampering down toward the village, the others in tow.

The courtyard was filled to capacity. The villagers all seemed to have a common quality to their look, their faces out of fashion, the kind that isn't seen around anymore except for really old pictures or portraits. They hadn't yet noticed Lee and the others and were engaged in various kinds of games and contests. One station offered contestants a chance to test their marksmanship by spitting apricot seeds into small holes dug in the ground a few feet away. At another stop they had a pushing contest, in which couples, one seated upon the shoulders of another, who was riding a unicycle, tried knocking each other off. More people were cheerfully throwing, pulling, pushing, jumping, ducking, and otherwise scrambling their way through different challenges. They were clearly having a marvelously good time.

Óseo jumped in to mingle with the crowd, dancing right alongside a group of villagers. They formed a circle, which contracted and expanded as they danced in and out with the jovial tempo of the music. A quartet of musicians stood on a tall podium at the far side of the courtyard, playing wind and string instruments made of wood. Óseo was holding hands with people on both sides and swinging them up and down as he pranced backwards and forwards, enjoying himself to no end.

"You're welcome to join your friend," an aged voice coming up from behind startled Lee and the others. An old woman reached out her spotted hand to Lee, who shook it and introduced herself and her friends.

"I'm Mayor Paskah," the woman said in a nasal voice. "But please feel free to call me Rosie."

She didn't look just old; she looked ancient, like her age was a matter of geology rather than biology. Her face was wrinkled the way sands are by the wind. Her hair came out her spotted scalp in coarse, wiry bundles, and her smile flashed a piano keyboard of teeth and gaps. Lee liked her right away.

"May I invite you to join us?" she said. "We always have visitors participate in our games—don't be shy, I positively insist."

"Ahem, well, madam." Percy didn't want to come across as a stuck-up, but he didn't want to play either. Madame Couronne had no qualms about making it clear that she was perfectly comfortable where she was, thank you very much, but that she would be ever so grateful if the Mayor would be kind enough to arrange for a fine-grade glass polish to be delivered to her. Mrs. Adocchiare, like Lee, seemed open to the idea of playing with the villagers. Lee didn't wait for Percy to finish putting together his excuse—she dragged him with her to the nearest game station, leaving her bag with Madame Couronne.

"Oh, you've chosen a good one. One of my favorites," said Rosie. "And don't be afraid to fall, the ground will catch you."

"Huh?" Lee didn't quite like the sound of that, but before she could find out what Rosie had meant, she was hoisted up by the villagers onto a pair of tall circus stilts. They made Lee more than three times as tall, and she could easily see the dark hilltops around the village. Each wooden stilt had a little footrest attached to the middle of it, just wide enough to accommodate her feet, and a round, flat paddle down below it, facing front. The stilts were fastened to her legs with straps around her thighs and ended shoulder high with black rubber handles.

She found herself above the cheering crowd facing Percy, who looked like an orange attempting to balance itself on chopsticks, Mrs. Adocchiare, who wobbled around but was surprisingly into the spirit of things, and Óseo, who'd joined them from the dancing circle, who seemed to have taken to the stilts as naturally as a stork to its own legs.

"The goal of the game is to bounce the ball to the other players using only your paddle," a curly-haired villager informed them, pointing to the paddles near the bottom of the stilts. "The last one standing who hasn't missed a serve of the ball is the winner!"

He took out a small ball, like a tennis ball only faded gray, and threw it up in the air. No sooner had it arced back down than Óseo boldly jumped to intercept it, kicking it over at Mrs. Adocchiare, who missed it by a mile.

"Oh, dear me," she said with an embarrassed laugh. "I don't think I'm very good at this game." A few people helped her off her stilts, and she remained to watch the rest of the game, giggling alongside Mayor Rosie.

Lee, who'd never particularly enjoyed playing sports, found that she really liked stiltball. She also decided that Óseo was the one to beat. After all, he had the unfair advantage of not having much weight to balance, and Percy would not be much more of a challenge than Mrs. Adocchiare.

The curly-haired villager threw the ragged ball up once more, and Óseo again made a dash after it, only this time Lee beat him to it. She jumped right between him and Percy, forcing them both to stop and teeter and nearly lose their balance, then managed to hit the ball with her paddle toward Óseo. He was quick on his stilts, however, and kicked it at Percy with high velocity. Percy succeeded in punting the ball back at him, but the play involved pivoting around one stilt, causing him to fall, and with an "Oh! Oh! Oohh!" down he came.

"This game will make you sore in two places," Rosie called out to him. "Your hide and your pride!" She gave a hearty laugh, as did Mrs. Adocchiare, and Lee, and Óseo, and everyone else around. Embarrassed, Percy tried to reestablish his cool. He grinned and quickly took off his stilts, dusted off his puffy pants, and joined the audience that had by now gathered around the game.

The third and last round was ready to begin. It was down to Lee and Óseo. The ball was thrown in the air, and the two went after it; both tried kicking it back up, but their stilts clashed, sending them staggering. Óseo was the first to regain balance, as much as Lee tried, and as the ball came back down, he spun around and kicked it toward the gap between her stilts. With more luck than skill, she crossed her legs at the exact right instant, blocking the ball's path with her paddles and ricocheting it back at Óseo like a missile. It didn't hit him with all that much force, but it didn't take much to topple a skeleton, she learned. Óseo crashed to the ground, sending bones flying all over. His head rolled near Percy, who picked it up.

"¡Caramba!" Óseo chuckled. "¿Qué sorpresa, eh? Je je je."

Percy held him up to eye level, grinning from fuzzy ear to fuzzy ear with satisfaction. He put Óseo's hat back on, bent down by his torso, and gently reattached his skull to his spine.

"Gracias, mi amigo," Óseo said in return.

"Are you okay?" Lee wanted to make sure.

"Sí, sí, niña." Óseo was now done plugging his arms and legs back in place with the help of some villagers and stood up. "Yu are very good. Maybe yu should think about making a career of it instead of painting, sí?" He winked at her, sending his boney hand through her hair. It tickled.

Mayor Rosie came over with Mrs. Adocchiare and Madame Couronne, whose jar was now polished to perfection and reflected the lights hanging above brilliantly.

"I've been told you've travelled far. You must be tired," she said. "Let's go to the Town Hall. We can talk more comfortably there."

Lee felt guilty, having allowed herself to be distracted with games while her father was waiting to be rescued. But truth be told, she was exhausted. She had no idea how long it had been since they left the room—she knew a day and a night had passed in this strange world, but it felt much longer. She wondered if time passed differently there, and if her mother had noticed she was gone. She didn't want her to worry.

Rosie took them to a house at the far end of the small village, which was no taller than the rest but was wider, with straw awnings above the doorway and windows. The inside was very plain; one bare lightbulb hanging at the center, a few benches in disorganized rows, and some small pillows thrown about, a couple large enough to sit on. Lee made herself comfortable. A few villagers joined them, and they all sat down more or less in a circle, except for Madame Couronne, who sat perfectly upright on one of the benches.

"Well," Rosie said, "you've seen what there is to see of our small village. We don't have much, but we make the most of it." She smelled like a moldy attic, full of secret treasures of the past. "And I do hope you've enjoyed our games. We're always happy to have guests come play with us."

"Yes, you've been a very gracious host indeed," said Percy, dutifully. "I do apologize for our arriving unannounced in the midst of your celebration."

"Nonsense," Rosie said, waving her veiny, spotted hand dismissively. "All we do here is play. There's always a party going on."

Lee loved the idea. She thought it was an excellent way to spend life after death.

"Is there no work to be done?" Percy arched a great eyebrow. "Surely, there's some serious business that needs attending to?"

"Oh, there are always things to do, of course, but why do they have to be serious?" Rosie smiled, revealing her crosswalk of teeth. "All of us here used to take our lives oh so seriously, back when we were alive. But then we grew up. Better late than never, huh?" The other villagers nodded happily, as did Percy, who realized it suited his spirit of adventure.

Rosie spread out her arms. "Besides, how can you really know someone until you've played a game with them?"

"Sí," Óseo said. He sat against the wall with one leg stretched out, playfully twiddling his rawboned toes, and looked at Lee, who was curled up in a giant pillow. "Yu should always take fun seriously and make fun of seriousness."

Lee agreed, but she put the thought aside. "Have you seen my father?" she asked Rosie and the other villagers. She hoped that Brevis was right.

"Possibly," said Rosie, suspending Lee's breath. "I'm sure we've seen many fathers. Though, come to think of it, we haven't had visitors in quite a while. What does your father look like?"

Lee tried to describe him as best she could; his hair, which was thick and wavy and the color of autumn, and his eyes, which were hazel and bright and had very few wrinkles around them. She struggled to describe him in as great detail as possible, but the words didn't quite come together. They weren't paints, they didn't form shapes or colors. So she decided to paint him instead.

She reached for her bag, which was on a nearby bench, and emptied its contents on the floor.

Rosie eyed her suspiciously. "People don't usually travel with luggage when they die—"

"Oh, I'm not dead." Lee was quick to clarify. "My dad is. I'm looking for him to bring him home."

Rosie and the other villagers looked skeptic, but Percy, Óseo, Madame Couronne, and Mrs. Adocchiare all nodded that it was true. "Huh. Well, give it time." Rosie flashed her checkered teeth.

Lee carefully set up her brushes and paints and leaned a canvas against a bench.

"I don't suppose you're alive too, are you?" Rosie said to the four. "You don't quite look it."

"I can't say that we are, madam," said Percy.

"Non," added Madame Couronne, "we have come here wiz ze ingénue." She gestured to Lee. "We have spent time wizout end imprisoned in a small room walled by darkness, until she came zrough her closet and brought us here."

"How odd!" Rosie bunched her wrinkly nose. "I've never heard of such a thing in my entire afterlife." She looked at Óseo, who was more interested in observing Lee than in the conversation they were having. "I suppose, then, that the jokey fellow is proof that even little girls have skeletons in their closet." She chuckled.

Lee summoned a new memory of her father: the bright winter Sunday when he'd taught her how to ride her bicycle. She was the last one in her old neighborhood to still have training wheels. So he bought a bike for himself, just so he could ride alongside her. They spent the morning riding around with only one training wheel, and at noon took off the other. She remembered being afraid and keeping her feet close to the ground, and, inevitably, falling and scraping her knee. Ron laughed at her, though mostly to help her laugh at herself. She considered crying at first, but she chose instead to climb back on, and by dusk she was riding her bike with little effort. Her dad looked so proud. She remembered that look very clearly and did her best to capture it.

When she was finished, she showed them the painting. Rosie and the other villagers revealed no sign of recognition.

"I'm afraid, terribly afraid, that we have not seen your father," said Rosie.

"That's okay." Lee looked down at her hands, covered in smudges of paint. She clenched and unclenched them; a mix of colors covered her palms now, making distinct each line that ran across them. "I'll find him."

"I believe you will." Rosie placed her spotted hand on Lee's. "You are a very special girl, Lee. You are *especially* special."

Lee grinned back. She liked the playful old lady, and her kind words sent a delicate wave of tickles down her back. She wiped her hands on her pajamas and packed up her paints. They were small tubes and already a quarter spent, but that would be enough. It was only a matter of time until a new way presented itself.

Rosie turned to Mrs. Adocchiare, who was sitting on the other side of her, leaning against a small mountain of pillows she had piled up. "Tell me—this room you were all trapped in, before the girl came—how did you get there? Were you someplace else beforehand?" She added, "It's very untraditional, you know."

Mrs. Adocchiare simply shrugged. "Oh, I have absolutely no idea, I'm sorry to say. Not an inkling. I passed away in my sleep, and when I woke up, I was in the room."

Rosie thought the matter over. "Well, it's a fine way to expire, as far as these things go, if you ask me. Lee, you should take an example from her."

Lee nodded in agreement, although she didn't see the point in worrying about the matter quite yet.

"And how about you?" Rosie moved on to Percy, who sat next in the circle, legs crossed. "I hope your passing was as pleasant?"

"The circumstances of my demise, madam, weren't quite as serene as Mrs. Adocchiare's, I'm afraid." He sighed.

Lee remembered Óseo had made a comment about Percy and a rhino when she first met them, but she was curious to learn more about what had happened.

Percy cleared his throat. "My vocation was that of explorer, trader, and fortune-hunter. I spent my adult life travelling the world, expanding my family's riches." He sat twiddling the tip of his great white mustache, staring out the window into the night sky. He cleared his throat again.

"I was on expedition to the African veldt. An untamable region of the Dark Continent, mind you. I fancied that I should search out some big game, perhaps a trophy to display upon my return home to England. And there it was…" He paused, inflating his bubble of a stomach with air like he was bracing himself. "The largest rhinoceros you have ever seen, I tell you, with a horn twice the size of a grown man's arm. It would have fetched a king's ransom."

Lee pursed her lips. She thought it was very cruel to hunt animals for sport. And it wasn't a sport at all—not unless the animal had a gun and knew how to use it, too. But she understood that Percy was of a different time, and people saw things differently back then.

"When the great beast was finally felled, I had my men take my photograph with it. But enough spirit remained in the confounded thing to toss me every which way, like a ragdoll! And that is how I met my end." He remained still, gazing out at the stars. "I had forgotten that money is merely something for man to make; it does not make a man. And in my zeal, I had become unmade myself." He lowered his head, knitting his shaggy eyebrows into a hard knot. "And I had left behind… the most precious of treasures."

"Your wife," Rosie said, knowingly.

"Lady Wordsworth," Percy whispered, as if the name itself required delicate handling. "My darling Felicity."

"What was she like?" Lee said.

Percy gave her a wistful smile. "Oh, she was a most attractive woman; her figure was rather tall and slender, her step light and firm, her whole appearance expressive of health and animation. Her deep brown eyes never lacked a twinkle. She set my heart ablaze and my soul aloft! And all she ever asked of me were my affections. But I… I'd been around her for so long that I couldn't even see her. I had come to take her for granted. I neglected my duty to her as husband, like a gardener who fails to water his prized flower." He crossed his arms deep into his chest, as if he was cold, or as if cradling a wound. "Oh, I am fortune's fool!"

Lee's eyes watered with Percy's heartache.

"Now, now, you mustn't cry," said Percy, leaning over and wiping her eye off with the back of his hand. "What's gone and what's past help should be past grief. Besides," he continued on a lighter note, "she indubitably went on to gad about town, squandering away my fortune."

She couldn't help but smile again. She was happy to. She didn't like being so quick to tear.

"For every route we choose to take, zere are many we leave behind, and many more we will ignore ahead. And only at ze end of each do we know if it was ze right choice or not," Madame Couronne advised. "But if you are wise, Lee, you will learn from ozers' journeys to make better choices in your own."

Lee took her advice to heart, though she was a little surprised that Madame Couronne cared enough to dispense it. Perhaps she had misjudged the woman.

"And how did your path lead you to the room, Madame?" said Rosie. She was like a kind great-grandmother, Lee thought, whose wits hadn't dampened but sharpened with age.

"I was a member of ze aristocracy of France—a Duchess of ze royal court of King Louis!" she declared with an air of pride, making sure all present were duly and sufficiently impressed. Even if she hadn't been sitting on a bench, with her head raised on a pillow, she would have been looking down on them. "Zen ze Terror began. All ze commoners—ze simpeltons, ze peasants, ze paupers, and all ze ozer wretches—zey toppled ze monarchy." She said this as if it were a thing too outrageously absurd to consider. She was obviously displeased with the turn of events. "And zat is how I left ze world, wiz a swift kiss of ze révolution's guillotine upon ze back of my neck."

Rosie looked at Madame Couronne, unsure how best to respond. The rest of the village council exchanged whispers.

"A distasteful spectacle, to be sure, and for which you have my sympathies." Rosie tried to sound as gracious as possible. "But doesn't this go to show that people should be allowed to govern themselves?"

"Of course not." Madame Couronne scoffed at the silly notion. "Ze masses cannot govern zemselves any more zan a flock of sheep can—zey need a shepherd, n'est-ce pas?"

"And what happens," Rosie prodded, "if bad people are doing the shepherding?"

"It is positively meaningless to divide people into 'good' and 'bad'—people are always both. But zey are eizer charismatic or dull. Great leaders are charismatic," Madame Couronne clarified.

Lee considered this for a moment, arriving at the conclusion that she did not at all agree. Goodness meant greatness, not the other way around. But Madame Couronne wasn't really bad. She was just... pompous. Although Lee had never met royalty before, it could very well be that all crowned heads were like that. Maybe it was even expected of them.

"Ah, I see," said Rosie, in a way that meant she didn't see at all. "And you, sir?" She turned to Óseo in hopes that he would prove more entertaining.

Óseo until then was sitting on the ground with his back against the wall, his hat slanted forward over most of his skull. He seemed perfectly happy to have remained outside the conversation.

"¿What can I say, señora? Cuando toca, toca—when it's yur time, it's yur time. I guess I'm just bad tu the bone, sí? Je je je je je."

"Oh, do tell." Rosie chuckled.

Óseo looked at Lee beside him; she looked back in eagerness.

"Bien. I was scared tu death—I jumped out of my skin. ¡Je je je je je je!"

Lee laughed, and Óseo put on an expression of satisfied amusement.

Rosie smiled. "As Madame Couronne said, we all have our paths. If yours steers clear of seriousness, Óseo," she said without a trace of judgment in her voice, "I hope it leads you to happiness. We certainly appreciate the value of that here." She waved her hand at the villagers behind her, who all nodded in agreement.

Lee turned her head back to Óseo. For an instant, the cheerful glint of his eye sockets was gone.

"Gracias, Señora," he said in a low voice, more to himself than to Rosie. He remained silent for a short time afterwards. "I hope so tu."

Lee looked to her companions, since they had known him far longer than she had. Their expressions indicated it was a subject best left alone.

"Well, well," said the Mayor, in a more cheerful tone. "So tell me, Lee, where were you thinking of looking for your father next?"

She had absolutely no idea. Not a clue. Not even an idea of where to look for a clue.

"We were given to understand, madam," Percy said, "that we are Nowhere, and that we should seek out Elsewhere. Am I correct?"

"Well, you're certainly Nowhere. But that's all there is around here, far as I know. And I've been here for quite a while, let me tell you." Rosie glanced back to the village council, who had remained silent, to see if any of them might know what, or where, Percy was referring to. They didn't.

"So where can my dad be? Where can we look for him?" Lee persisted.

"Well…" Rosie thought hard, folding the squiggly wrinkles of her face together. "I'm afraid I am not young enough to know everything there is to know. But I agree—if he is not here, he has got to be Elsewhere."

"And how do you propose we find the place?" said Percy.

"That I do not know," Rosie confessed, "but I do know this—the places beyond here are no places to walk about. They're fraught with peril, for all of you, but particularly for you, Lee." Rosie was severe now, a startling change from her casual demeanor. "The lands of the dead are no place for a little live girl. Go back home, Lee, while you still can."

Lee's heart rattled against her ribcage like a heavy load of coins in a piggybank.

"Oh, dear me! Perhaps we should reconsider?" Mrs. Adocchiare said. Percy, Óseo, and Madame Couronne seemed equally apprehensive.

"No! I'm not running away," Lee cried. "I'm looking for my dad. I came here to get him back, and I'm not leaving until I find him."

Despite her bold display of courage, she had to fight off the impulse to run back to her closet and to her mom. But she was also doing this for her. She couldn't go back emptyhanded.

"Stouthearted child…" Rosie shook her head between disappointment and admiration.

Lee looked at Óseo with imploring eyes. She needed at least one of her friends to encourage her.

"I have found that the best way tu give advice tu children is tu find out what they want tu do, and then advise them tu do exactly that." He winked at her his mischievous wink, which had yet to fail to make her smile.

And with that, it helped enlist the resolve of first Percy, then Mrs. Adocchiare, and finally Madame Couronne. She felt grateful for the loyalty of her friends.

She spent a restless night curled up on her large pillow next to her father's painting, sleeping sometimes, then waking, and wondering, and falling back asleep. Rosie and the villagers had left the house to return in the morning. The others slept effortlessly, in spite of Madame Couronne's sharp snores echoing through her jar. In her short episodes of wakeful slumber, Lee saw the stars outside the window slowly disappear, until all that remained was blackness. But she was far too tired to truly notice it, and at some point she managed to fall into a dreamless sleep.

An earsplitting, thunderous racket shook her, and she jumped to her feet. It had startled the others, too. They all looked around in alarm. There was no more small house. There was no more village. There were no more green hills. They were Elsewhere.

V

A second deafening roar and Lee and the others were coiled up, back to back, ready to spring at the first sign of danger. Lee surveyed the landscape around them: a large clearing amidst tall bare trees. There was nothing else.

Another shuddering noise, this time closer. It resonated through the woods around them, filling the spaces between the trees with bedlam. Lee listened carefully, trying to determine what it could be and where it was coming from.

Another noise. It sounded like nothing she had ever heard before, loud and mad and raging. Percy grabbed her hand. His eyes narrowed.

"What? What is it?" she said.

"We best not find out. Come along—make haste," he said in a very efficient voice.

He held onto her and led them into the thicket.

"¿Percival?" Óseo stepped lively by.

Percy whispered back, so Lee couldn't hear. But she did. "War."

They made their way through barren trees and bushes away from the ruckus, going deeper and deeper into the forest. Sad browns and sepias of rusted undergrowth and decaying branches surrounded them. This is where dead trees go, she thought.

It was sweltering. The air was hot and humid, burning inside her chest with each labored breath. She was drenched in sweat, beads trickling their way down her back, making her regret wearing long-sleeve flannel pajamas and bootie slippers. She looked up. There was no sign of a sun.

They continued in a quick, steady pace until they couldn't hear anything. The forest was now silent. There was no wind or birds or small mammals climbing trees. The only sound came from their footsteps crushing the shriveled foliage on the ground. And Lee's rumbling stomach. It was still doing its thinking in real-world time, apparently, and it was now making itself heard. The four looked at her in puzzlement.

"¡Voto al chápiro! ¿Niña, what du yu have in there? It sounds like an angry volcano demanding its virgin sacrifice." Óseo snickered.

"I'm sorry," she muttered, embarrassed. "I'm hungry. Haven't eaten anything since I left home."

"Then we'll look for something for you to eat, dear. I'm sure we'll find something," Mrs. Adocchiare said, looking around the dead woodland.

"I haven't had a bite to eat in ages myself, come to think of it," Percy said. "Nor do I require it. But a spot of tea and a scone do sound scrumptious."

They continued on farther into the thickening woods. The forest clasped its branches around them, the shade providing little relief from the heat. They made their way over protruding roots and under low-hanging limbs and through prickly twigs, their line of sight limited to only a few yards ahead. A sense of horror increasingly tugged at Lee: Despite the eerie quietude, she could feel things lurking in the shadows, following them, ready to jump out at any moment.

A sudden movement at her periphery caught her attention, but before she could warn the others, two large shadows leaped out at them.

"¡*Cáscaras!*" Óseo cried out, instinctively reaching back to shield her.

"I give you fair warning, whoever you are. You—" Percy began to say.

"Friends. We are friends, sir!" One of the characters stepped forward slowly, showing his empty, white-gloved hands. "We are friendly, favorable, and fond, even if not familiar. I pledge my perdurable promise most persistently, people."

Lee thought that anyone who spoke like that couldn't be all that bad.

Percy was not entirely convinced. "Who are you?"

"I am known, far and wide, as the rapturous, crowd-rousing, resplendent—and, if I do say so myself, quite ravishing—Ringmaster Phineas," he announced with pride.

Lee looked him over. He was a strange man, with a head unnecessarily large for his body. Fuzzy moss covered the left side of his face, from the corner of his bloodshot eye down his collar. Like Percy, he had a moustache, but his was much smaller and black. He wore a black stovepipe hat with a wide burgundy sash around it, matching his faded tailcoat, which was missing a tail. The coat had a row of large gold buttons on each side with thin golden cords holding them together, and golden strips ran down the sides of his black pants.

"Oh, you're a circus impresario? How nice," Mrs. Adocchiare said with childlike glee.

"Sadly and sorrowfully," he replied with puckered lips, "no more. My marvelously mesmerizing, merry-making menagerie was mandatorily drafted into the Queen's miscreant military for the miserable war."

"Oh, dear me," Mrs. Adocchiare said.

Percy looked concerned. He wanted to stay as far away from any fighting going on as possible. Madame Couronne didn't seem too thrilled with the idea either.

"And who's this, then?" Percy pointed his chin at the man behind Ringmaster Phineas.

"Ahh!" he replied. "Ladies and gentlemen—allow me to introduce the spectacular, stupendous, senses-shattering sensation—Sõt the Gypsy!"

"'allo." The man stepped forward, offering something between a nod and a shrug. His head rested on his collar without the benefit of a neck. He had a moustache as well, but his went all the way up his jaws and connected to his sideburns, like a giant W. He wore a red bandana and big hoop earrings and a black vest over a purple shirt and a yellow sash tied around his middle. His pants were brown, and his boots looked like a pirate's, with the broad flap around the top. But despite the outfit, he didn't look to Lee all that spectacular or sensational.

"I am Sõt." His voice was broad and crusty. "And this is Sulyok." A little monkey, with a white mask of fur and pointy ears, climbed up his back and perched itself on his shoulder. It wore a little black vest that matched Sõt's.

"Monkey!" Lee hopped over all excited, but the animal pulled itself up on its hindlegs, exposing two rows of sharp fangs, and spat out a "*hisssssssssssss!*" She quickly retreated.

"Please forgive Sulyok." Sõt shooed him back down. "I found him in the woods—he's not used to human company. I was thinking of adding him to my act. Put him in a wooden barrel or something like that, like when they say 'funnier than a barrel of monkeys,' you know? I know they say 'monkeys,' so it has to be more than one to be funny, but a regular wooden barrel will only hold two, or three if they're crammed in there, and even then only for a moment. So I'm looking for a big barrel, if you see one, because if I have one that's big enough, really big, I could put more monkeys in it. It'd be a bit loud, I guess, and lots of chaos, and probably messy, with monkeys liking to fling their poop around and all, but that should be really funny, right?" he said in one breath. He was met with five unblinking stares. "Maybe if they were wet monkeys?" He tried for another option.

"Mon dieu! What in ze world is zis imbécile blabbering about?" Madame Couronne cried. "If I have to listen to zis one minute longer my head will explode."

"Well, if yur head blows up, at least the mess will stay contained in the jar, sí? Je je je je." Óseo seemed exceptionally pleased with himself. She looked daggers at him.

"We can't linger here any longer," Ringmaster Phineas said. "Sõt and I are wanted men—declared disloyal defectors by the dastardly Queen. We've dodged the draft, and now we avoid detection by hiding in the dense woods. We must depart before we are discovered."

Madame Couronne, Óseo, Mrs. Adocchiare, Percy, and Lee all followed Sõt, Sulyok, and Ringmaster Phineas through the dim growth.

"We are in search of—" Percy started.

"My dad," Lee continued.

"Where would we go about looking for him?" Percy finished.

"Pretty princess," Ringmaster Phineas turned to Lee without slowing down, "have you lost your precious parent?"

"Yes."

"Then we shall take you to the town at the tip of the tree line. If anyone would have a clue, it would be the crazy cantankerous crones who live there."

"Thank you, thoroughly and, um, thoughtfully." She expressed her gratitude in kind. He gave her a pleased grin and jolted ahead through a tangle of hanging vines.

He was a quick man and walked with a jerking rhythm, practically in skips. His gaze constantly flashed from side to side, back and forth, keeping an eye out for the people that were after him.

He and Sõt led them over terrain that didn't allow much for upright walking. They marched on fast, though, and the woods reluctantly let them through. Hours into the hot day, they finally reached the edge of the woods.

"We cannot conceivably continue beyond this crest." Ringmaster Phineas stopped in place. "Out of concern of being captured. But we wish you a favorable, fruitful, and fortunate search for your father, princess!"

He took off his tall hat, presented Sõt and Sùlyok for an encore, and the three of them disappeared back into the dark woods.

"Good luck," she called after them, but the forest gave no response.

The trees ended not gradually but in a straight line, like an immense wall, at a waterfront that extended beyond their view on both sides. The water was as thick and black as liquid marble, more oozing than flowing. Its surface evaporated in the heat, creating a thick mist that filled the air all around. Mrs. Adocchiare pointed to a small stone bridge further downstream, and they crossed it toward the town beyond.

VI

The town was large, made up of many houses and streets and empty spaces. There was not a soul in sight. It was completely deserted, as silent as the woods they had just come from. The air was cooler but heavy, burdened with damp rot and bitter dust that made it difficult to breath. Lee felt nauseated.

"Such a rank odour." Percy scrunched his nose.

The sky was gray, a flat haze like a sheet of frosted glass hanging over them. Different size pools of murky liquid collected on the cobblestone. Lee looked around carefully. Nothing stirred but some tattered drapes, fluttering in the few windows that weren't shut tightly or boarded up.

They crossed through the town, not a word spoken between them. Lee was in no mood to lead them into conversation. This was a place of sadness, and hers was great. She thought of her father, and where he might be, and how he might be feeling. Of all her regrets, the things she never got to do with him or say to him. She never even said goodbye. She hoped to find him soon, to return home with him to her mom and Ron, who missed him just as terribly.

Eventually, they came upon an open space at what seemed to be the heart of town. A broken fountain stood at its center; a host of marble cherubs, now chipped and fractured, hung motionless in mid-flight, looking down on Lee and the others. The dense mist filled the large square, rolling along the ground like a cloud of smoke, billowing upwards.

"Lugubre...." Madame Couronne said quietly.

"Sí," Óseo agreed. "Esta muy lúgubre. This favela is forsaken, niña. We will not find clues tu where yur father is here."

Lee reluctantly agreed, when a faint whispering caught her ear. She looked around—there was no one in sight. The hushed voice seemed to come from a street that intersected with the square under a large archway. She moved toward it.

"¿Niña…?" Óseo wondered, but she didn't respond. He and the others followed.

She crossed the square and neared the arch. The whisper now sounded a little less faint but still incoherent:

It was a dry and dusty town, the sun rose harsh, no rain fell down

Their feet were blistered, their hands were flayed

The mining went hard, but it certainly paid.

While small and shallow was the cavern they missed

Its walls yielded freely many riches that shined.

The three became brothers through purpose and friendship

On their journey back home, they laughed at past hardship

For the treasure they packed, they had a single desire

To provide for their families, for all they require.

The youngest turned to his brethren, they'd been through so much

He tried to express how he felt, but no words came as such.

He was a simple miner, he didn't have the words

So he shot them both dead and left them to the birds.

Lee walked around the corner and found herself facing a small man with a big, almost perfectly round head. His legs were bowed, twiggy things, peaking from under a wide robe that covered him to his knees. It was white with broad horizontal stripes of dark purple, and was soiled with every shade of brown, gray, and black. The man was as hairless as a dolphin, aside from a single thick eyebrow that roofed both his eyes. His face was dark with a cake of dust sticking to his sweat, except for two streaks that ran from beneath his eyes, down his cheeks, and met at his chin—the path his tears kept clean.

Lee looked at the giant plank of wood that sat atop his shoulders, two pieces held together with a series of iron locks, his head and hands dangling out of holes in the middle. A similar, smaller board held his ankles, forcing him to shuffle in mincing steps. He walked down the street toward Lee, swaying his body from side to side.

"Hi there," Lee said, as cheerfully as possible.

He lifted his eyes and smiled at her, expression vacant.

"I think I heard you singing. Am I right? Were you singing a song?" she asked.

He stared at her for a moment, then nodded.

"Well, you can keep singing, if you want to. I'd love to hear it."

He looked at her, and at the four behind her, and gave a slow nod. He took a minute, and started, in a soft, whispering voice:

It was a dry and dusty town, the sun rose harsh, no rain fell down

Their feet were blistered, their hands were flayed

The mining went hard, but it certainly paid.

While small and shallow was the cavern they mined

Its walls yielded freely many riches that shined.

The three became brothers through purpose and friendship

On their journey back home, they laughed at past hardship.

For the treasure they packed, they had a single desire;

To provide for their families, for all they require.

The youngest turned to his brethren, they'd been through so much

He tried to express how he felt, but no words came as such.

He was a simple miner, he didn't have the words

So he shot them both dead and left them to the birds.

Lee didn't know quite what to make of it. She felt very sorry for him, but she also suspected that he was the young man in the ballad, and that was why he was locked up in stocks. And if that was the case, it was punishment well deserved.

"How... droll," Madame Couronne critiqued.

"Interesting balada. What du yu call it?" asked Óseo.

The small man in the big stocks looked back. "*Mine.*"

"I say, sir—we're looking for a few elderly ladies who are supposed to live around here. Might you know where we may find them?" Percy said.

The miner nodded and turned one of his confined hands to point at a street that ran under another archway.

They thanked him for his help and wished him all the best.

The other end of town was no different, crumbling and decayed. It was a ghost town long abandoned by its ghosts. They walked down the street, which the width of an alleyway but the length of an avenue, made of small, narrow houses huddled together as if for warmth, with a *tick-tick-tick* made by Óseo's foot bones against the cobblestones.

Past the outskirts the streets turned into roads, winding up and down across barren hilltops, gradually disappearing into the earth. A small number of trails ended under a cluster of trees close by, where stands, carts, and makeshift booths made for a small marketplace. All the stands stood empty but three, which were occupied by three impossibly old ladies, presenting large heaps of red, green, and yellow apples.

Lee's ravenous hunger rolled and rumbled around her insides. Her mouth watered.

"Ooh la la!" Madame Couronne patted her back. "You are very hungry, non?"

She nodded and walked over to the old ladies and their apples.

"Pardonnez-moi, Mesdames," Madame Couronne said, approaching their stands with a polite smile. "Have you apples to sell for ze girl?"

One of the old women, who had a lipless mouth and a few renegade hairs popping out of her chin, raised her gnarled hand to her ear in painstakingly slow motion. "Vhat? I no hear vell. Vhat you say?"

"We would like to buy some of your apples," Madame Couronne repeated in a loud voice.

"Ah!" The ancient-looking woman nodded. "Yes, yes. You take vhat you vant, yes?"

Lee reached out eagerly but then stopped. She had no way of paying.

"Don't vorry," the woman said. "I give you gift. You eat mine apples, yes?"

"Vhy? Vhy she have to eat *your* apples? Mine are better. She take mine!" The old lady at the adjacent stand waved her chappy fingers at Lee to come over.

"Pffah!" The third one spat out. "Vhere she get her apples—you two? She von't like vhat apples you sell. Come little girl, I give you best apples."

Lee was confused. The weird old women didn't seem to mind giving her their fruit free of charge; they just didn't want her to get it from one of the others.

"Why do you not just sell different types of apples?" Madame Couronne tried to make peace. "*You* sell ze red apples, *you* sell ze green apples, and *you* sell ze yellow apples, oui?"

"Vhat you talking about? This is no vay to sell. Then the customers buying only the color apples they vant. This vay they have selection with each of us. And I show mine apples are best as vell!" said the old lady in the middle cart.

"You vish." The one on the right, the first one, scoffed. "I vill prove—you eat mine, yes?"

Lee wasn't quite sure what to do. She didn't want to offend any of them, but her stomach threatened to fling her into one of the applecarts if she didn't eat something right away.

"How about this, then," Percy said, intervening, "the girl will accept apples from each of you, so she may enjoy each of your generosity, hmm?"

The old women grudgingly consented, giving Lee their finest reds, yellows, and greens, which she stuffed into her bag, making it heavy.

"These, I hope, should sate your appetite," said Percy.

Lee took an apple, a red one, and ate it. It had a bitter taste, like the smell of old trees, and a texture like dried-up sponge. But she was starving and didn't care.

She finished the apple and went on to devour a second, a third, and, to the astonishment of her friends, a fourth. The three old vendors seemed very pleased.

"I tell you vhat," said the cranky old lady with the creaky joints. "You thirsty, yes? Vant I should give you to drink pickle juice from jar? It makes vonders for body and spirit."

"No, thank you." She shook her head. It didn't sound terribly appealing, even though she was parched. She thought the old lady looked like she came out of a pickle jar herself.

"No, no, Mincha!" the old woman to Lee's left cried out with dissatisfaction. "I svear—you and Atara mine sisters, but I the one vich got all the brains. You give the girl some vater. Yes?" she asked Lee.

Lee nodded.

"And then," she continued, "I also vill give you real food, not only apples. Mine favorite; you have melted goose fat vith crispy bits of skin—it vondeful!"

The description took care of whatever was left of Lee's appetite.

"Guta, this not vhat she vants," said Atara, wagging her toothless jaw. "You are vhat you eat, yes? Stay vith fruit." She waved a long bony finger that took off in a different direction at every joint.

"Don't be silly, you old crone. Stop scaring the girl." Guta gestured her shriveled hand in dismissal. "She young and healthy. I vouldn't vorry."

"Vait a minute. You calling *me* old? You mine older sister, you decaying cadaver!"

"Pffah!" the third joined in. "Vhat you two mummified biddies know? You not even have the good apples. Your red apples are sour and your green apples are sveet!"

"Blah! You think your apples so much best, Mincha, I hope your mouth never closes to them and your backside never opens for them," said Atara.

"Oh-hooo! You think you something special? Hot, skinless peppers should climb up your noses," said Guta.

"Yes? May a balcony fall on your head," said Mincha.

"May another hump grow on your back," said Guta.

"May all your teeth fall out, except of one to give you horrible toothache," said Atara.

"May vorms hold big vedding in your stomach and invite relatives from all over," said Mincha.

"May your soul reincarnate into a cat surrounded by dogs," said Guta.

"I vish you find Ali-Baba's cave vith treasure, and your arms and legs fall off," said Atara.

Lee, Percy, Madame Couronne, Mrs. Adocchiare, and Óseo all exchanged glances.

"These brujas are muy loco, sí?" Óseo whispered through the side of his mouth.

Lee agreed. They certainly weren't the cheerful types.

"Ahem!" Percy cleared his throat as loud as he could. The two arches of his mustache spread out like the wings of a sparrow. "I beg your pardon, madams. We are most grateful for your kindness. And if we may trouble you yet again, we were told you may be able to assist us in locating a gentleman. The girl's father."

"Hmm. Been long vhile from vhen I see new men. They all drafted in army. There is var going on, yes?" said Guta.

The thought of her father being hurt suddenly occurred to Lee. Finding him became more urgent than ever.

"Why is there a war?" she asked.

The three old women shook their heads.

"Ve have vitnessed the chaos and the conflict and the destruction everyvhere, but ve not know vhy it is. Best you should be careful. It very dangerous."

"Pffah! Vhat do you know, you moldy hag." Mincha sneered. "Little girl, you know you looking Elsvhere, yes?"

"Yes."

"Your father pass avay only now, yes?"

"Yes."

"Vell, you not in right place. You should go on the other side, after the varzone. There is vhere the new dead go."

Percy didn't seem to care for the idea at all. Mrs. Adocchiare didn't seem much of a fan either.

"No, no. Ignore mine harpy of sister. She give bad directions. You vant to find your father? If he come here, he is in one of the armies," said Guta.

"Both you crumbling gargoyles are confusing to the girl!" said Atara. "Elsvhere is very big place. If your father is far avay, you have to valk around the fighting. But if he is close, he probably is in army. You ask from King and Qveen to know. Understand?"

Lee understood. She also understood that she wasn't any closer to finding her dad than when she started this journey.

Percy took a deep breath and looked at her. "Young lady, I shall talk to you without any reserve, because I am sure you are as well able to understand me as many older persons would be." She found herself alarmed by his grave tone. "If you seek my advice, I suggest, *strongly,* that we circumvent the hostilities taking place and make our way to whatever awaits us beyond. I have witnessed the horrors of combat firsthand, and I do not at all wish for you to experience them."

Lee gazed down at the gray earth.

"However," he continued, "we have all sworn to follow you on your quest. And so it is your decision, young lady, whether we march ahead or not."

Her heart beat like the chugging of a speeding train. She didn't know exactly what to expect, but she knew war was a very, very dangerous thing. And all she was armed with were her luck and her wits. She wondered if she had enough of either. She looked over to the mountain terrain ahead and thought of her father, somewhere out there. She pulled herself up to her full height. She clenched her jaw. She steadied herself.

"Straight ahead." She did her best to keep her voice from trembling.

Percy sighed. "Very well then."

They prepared to leave. Madame Couronne, who was carefully leaning against a ramshackle booth, stood up and brushed the dust from the back of her dress.

"Thank you for all your help, ladies." Mrs. Adocchiare smiled at the three old women. "Could you, please, also direct us to the nearest source of water?"

The three pointed three crooked fingers as one to a dip in the ground farther down the road.

A small brook ran between the highest and lowest points of where two curves of the ground met. Clear water gushed out, bright and sparkling in the light and making the most wonderful flowing sound.

"This should quench yur thirst, eh, niña?" Óseo said.

Lee put her head in the water, letting the frosty stream splash against her forehead and run down her face. She cupped her hands tightly together, creating a small pool of perfectly transparent water, and drank her fill of the satisfying fluid.

They sat down on the rocks and rested themselves for a bit. Picking up another two apples from her bag, both green, Lee took a giant crunchy bite out of the first. She chewed on it, slowly, savoring every bite. Suddenly, she noticed that the others were staring at her. She looked back, her cheeks stuffed to capacity like a chipmunk's. They smiled. She returned a baffled look. Then she understood: she held out her arm and offered them an apple. But they simply shook their heads and smiled some more, all four of them.

"No, gracias," Óseo said. "Eating is no longer necessary tu our continued existence. We were just remembering how it was tu eat. Sometimes it is hard tu recall the memory."

Lee swallowed her bite quickly. "How... how does it feel? Not to be alive? To be dead?"

"Hmm." Mrs. Adocchiare gave it some thought. "It's hard to crumple into words. I suppose it's a little like the taste of an apple—it can't really be explained, it can only be experienced. But you shouldn't be in any hurry to find out, eh, dear?"

Lee agreed. They rested for a little while longer, then continued on their way.

VII

They walked across ground that rose to high peaks and dipped to deep gorges like the waves of a stormy ocean. For the most part they kept to the middle, where, according to Percy, they had the best advantage of being able to see far enough without being seen too easily. They passed fields that still bore the scars of battle. Burnt and broken wreckage of machinery and tools peppered the land like seashells on a shore. Ravens shrieked. But there were no people anywhere.

It took hours to get from one point to the next. Time stretched and yawned. Dusk tinted everything in blue, bringing with it a cool mountain breeze. They followed a winding path between the mountains, a trail of flat soil just wide enough for them to pass. After a while the road leveled off, which allowed them to pick up their pace considerably, until it dropped once again, into a narrow ravine. There was enough light to see what was closely in front of them, but not where the gulch ended. They walked it at a safe pace, with Lee and Percy in the lead.

Halfway through the ravine, they came across a group of people silhouetted against the rock walls.

"Hello there," the dark figure standing in the middle said.

"Good evening," Percy said, cautiously.

The man tilted his head to the side.

"Umm… hello," Lee said, trying to sound friendly.

There were four men, including the one who spoke, and they spread themselves across the path. Lee then heard movement behind her—she turned around to see four more men, walking toward them. They weren't trying to sneak up. They walked the way a spider glides down a vibrating web strand.

"I am Alichino," the man finally said, slowly tilting his head the other way. "Perhaps you've heard of me? I am a… collector, for the Queen."

"Bounty hunter, you mean to say." Percy looked back at him daringly.

The man smiled, and Lee's blood curdled. Now that her eyes had sufficiently adjusted to the dark, she could see his face was a coal-black mask, which covered all but his jaw. His mouth had no skin around it, leaving dark, red flesh exposed. She could see the wet muscle and sinew. Underneath the mask, she realized, he had no face. He was horrifying.

"It's a living," he said, with a full sense of irony.

Percy stood his ground. "And I suppose you'll be taking us to this Queen of yours, will you?"

Alichino smiled again, revealing old teeth.

Lee took Percy's hand and gave him a subtle nod.

"Oh, bloody hell." Percy huffed. "Friends," he turned to Mrs. Adocchiare, Madame Couronne, and Óseo, who all stood petrified. "We shall go with this fiendish character and his band of louts. And we shall have an audience with the monarch."

Alichino smiled.

The ravine ended at the foothills of a massive slope, which they had to climb up one side of and down the other before they walked onto an open field. Under the brighter starlit sky Lee could now see Alichino in greater detail. He wore a tight, full-body suit made of triangular patches, all faded to different shades of grays and blacks; his spine protruded through his back in ridges as he walked, giving him a wiry, insectile look. She found him both repulsive and terrifying, and hoped her father didn't cross paths with him.

"So," Óseo said. "Yu and yur troupe roam the countryside capturing people, sí? ¿That is what yu du?"

"Fugitives," he answered. "Deserters, like you. And like your friends in the woods. Or didn't you think I knew about them?" He hovered at the edge of each sentence as he spoke. "Don't worry. Their day will come soon."

"But don't you care about what people want?" Lee couldn't help herself. "What if they don't want to be in your stupid army anyway?"

Alichino clicked his tongue a slow "*tch tch*," indicating "no."

They walked the rest of the way in utter silence under a canopy of stars but no moon.

Before long they arrived at the Queen's army camp, a square grid of patched tents, all the same size, spread across a large, sandy area. Tall wooden spikes stood by each tent and around the camp's perimeter, from which hung lanterns of different shapes and sizes and brightness. There were hundreds of them, like a swarm of fireflies hovering about the underbrush.

Alichino and his seven goons led them through the guarded gate and between the tents, making sure the new captives were seen by all. Inquisitive and eager eyes peered from every inch of space, whispering among themselves. All this was mostly lost on Lee, who was busy scanning the worn faces in search of her father. If he was there, he was nowhere to be seen.

As they passed the crowd cleared the way, and she could see that it consisted of not only men, but also elders, and women, and even children—some no older than herself. They were all dead, she realized, and wondered why they'd died, and if they remembered the loved ones they'd left behind. Óseo, as he walked along, lifted his hat to each of the women.

"Ze sin and wickedness of ze lower orders in zis place is frightful." Madame Couronne sneered. "Not one person here looks civilized."

They approached a large tent, several times the size of the others, decorated in gold, silver, and royal blue flourishes, with an awning extending above its entrance. Guards surrounded the tent, forming a circle that ended in a row of sentries on each side of its entrance. It was a tent befitting a Queen.

Alichino ushered them in. They entered as a cluster, with Percy and Madame Couronne at Lee's side.

The inside of the tent was extremely spacious, and if Lee didn't know any better, she'd swear it was larger than the outside. Ornate lanterns hung down its poles, flickering with candlelight. In the rear was a large, thick-cushioned red velvet couch, on which sat the Queen, luxuriating like a Persian cat.

She was gargantuan in size, large enough to fill four bathtubs, Lee estimated. Deep rolls of fat cascaded from her neck downwards, expanding until they spread across the couch, hiding her feet in their folds. Her shimmering gold dress stretched across her oversized frame and draped over the edge of the couch, giving her the shape of a melting pyramid. She looked down at them, unimpressed.

"Begone, you." She waved the back of her hand at Alichino, who bowed deeply and retreated out the doorway without turning around.

Madame Couronne and Mrs. Adocchiare bowed down and Percy and Óseo kneeled. Lee offered a curtsy. She tried not to look at the Queen directly, but her immense shape filled her field of vision.

"Yeeees?" the Queen said.

"Your Majesty," Percy said with reverence. "If I may supplicate you for assistance, we—"

"You most certainly may *not*."

Lee looked at the Queen. Her mouth was an angry slit.

"*We* are the Queen, and *you* are our subjects. *You* do not ask things of *us*; you do *our* bidding. Have we made ourselves *clear*?"

Her voice was a series of high-pitched tremors. Lee was puzzled by her referring to herself as "we." She was certainly big enough for several people. It wasn't hard to figure out how she had died—obviously, she ate herself to death.

"Now. We understand that you were captured in the straits, heading back *toward* the camp. This seems an odd direction for runaways. We *demand* to know *why!*"

"Votre Majesté," Madame Couronne addressed her, one royal to another, "we beg your forgiveness; we are not renegades. We are strangers here—we are only looking for our friend's fazer."

The Queen looked mystified for a moment, then simply bored. "*Of course* you are. We knew this, naturally. We were simply *testing* your honesty."

"Of course, Your Excellency." Madame Couronne bowed.

"Which of you is missing a father? *You*?" She waved a plump, bejeweled hand at Mrs. Adocchiare.

"Um, no, ma'am. Me." Lee stepped forward.

The Queen twisted in her couch, which moaned under her weight.

"*Of course* it's you, you silly little thing." She rolled her eyes. She looked at Lee for a long moment, inspecting her from head to toe, unimpressed.

"You do not belong here, then. You are an outlander. But you are looking for your father *here*?"

Lee recognized that the Queen, having restated what was just told to her, believed she had drawn the conclusion herself.

"Yes, ma'a—Your Majesty. I think he might be in your army… If he is, ca—may I take him home, please?"

The Queen smiled at Lee, a smile that took all her concentration, as if she hadn't smiled in a very, very long time and had to drag it back up from deep memory.

"*Of course* you may. Just as soon as we win the war."

"But, but my dad isn't a soldier, he—he's just a dad. He doesn't—"

"Speak *clearly*, girl. No greatness has ever come of a *stutterer*!" The Queen frowned down her nostrils.

Lee struggled to find the right words to protest. Percy put his hand on her shoulder. It felt comforting.

"My dad doesn't know how to fight in a war. I'm sure you won't miss him. He's just one man, and your army is so huge."

The Queen smacked her lips and licked them with a small, strawberry-like tongue. Lee could tell her plea had fallen on deaf ears.

"Our war is a *holy* war. And each soldier is a holy warrior. *No one* is expendable! But let it be said that we are a benevolent monarch; when we have won our war, you may have your father back."

Percy kept his hand on Lee's shoulder, and this gave her the courage to persist.

"Is it almost over?"

The Queen threw back her head and roared laughing at the sky. "*Of course* not. Everyone fighting it is *already* dead, so we see no reason for them to stop. The war has been going on *forever*—and it's *far* too important to not *continue* forever!"

Lee was about to respond, and not at all politely, but Percy gently squeezed her shoulder.

"Your Majesty, begging your forgiveness, but may we inquire as to the nature of this conflict?" he said.

The Queen stretched her mouth in annoyance. "You are in the kingdom of Eponymia, of which *we* are the undisputed ruler. Our subjects are virtuous people, devoted to worshipping Ovo the almighty, he who presides over all—"

"Ovo?" Mrs. Adocchiare wondered.

"¡Oh-ho!" Óseo rattled his skull mockingly at her. "La beata is going tu argue religion now?"

Percy shushed them both. The Queen did not seem to notice the interruption. She was too busy expressing deep and profound disgust. "But, *tragically*, we suffer the misfortune of bordering with the kingdom of Shibbolet—a realm of godless heretics and blasphemers! Oh, *woe* is us." She shook her head with all the sorrow of the great catastrophe.

Lee pretended to nod seriously. "Can't you just be friends and believe in different things?"

"Don't be *preposterous*," the Queen sprayed in righteous fury. "It is not just our *right* but our *duty* to protect the honor of Ovo, the divine!"

"Why?" Lee asked.

"The Shibboletanians and their King worship the false god of *ovO*," she emphasized the difference, looking like she bit into a lemon. "You see, those heathens do their reading and writing from right to left. And everyone knows, *of course*, that it's *wrong* to begin at the right. It is a *travesty* to all that is sacred and holy!"

"Why?" Lee asked.

"*Why?!*" The Queen looked like she was about to explode. "Because their false idol is the exact *opposite* of the one, *true* Ovo. Theirs is the *Anti*-Ovo. *Obviously,* this is proof that their faith seeks to commit sacrilege and *destroy* ours. But *we* shall be the ones to destroy *their* dark devotion. *We* shall be victorious."

Lee wondered why so few adults ever made sense. Sure, they made a "this-is-because-of-that" sort of sense, but not real sense. Maybe that's why most adults spoke to children the way they did; maybe they thought that kids had the same sort of sense that they did, only less of it, instead of a sense of their own. The thought seemed sensible.

"Um, I have an idea…" she offered, cautiously. The Queen looked unimpressed. "What if everyone writes OVO in capital letters, instead of fighting over which

'O' to start from? That way it's the same from both sides, and everyone can get along."

Percy, Madame Couronne, Mrs. Adocchiare, and Óseo smiled with pride. The Queen, on the other hand, bellowed with laughter—chuckled and chortled and chattered until she almost choked. To Lee's disappointment, she didn't.

"You're positively *mad*," she howled, her rolls of fat quivering around her. "It's the most *ludicrous* idea we've ever heard!"

"I suppose, then, that peace talks are not in consideration?" Percy said dryly, to which the Queen was quick to respond, "Talk is the currency of *failure*."

"A sour disposition, that one, sí?" Óseo whispered into the back of Lee's ear.

"But it's only a name," Lee said. "It's just a word. What's the big difference if it's capital-O-v-o or o-v-capital-O or all-capitals OVO?"

"Indeed, Your Excellency, what's in a name?" Percy echoed.

The Queen looked at them both.

"There's nothing '*just*' about a word. A single word can make *all* the difference—you wouldn't say there's little distinction between a dragonfly and a dragon, now *would* you? Saying there's no difference between Ovo and ovO is like… like…" She searched for a fitting analogy. "It's like misspelling 'Bob' *seven* different ways!"

Lee and the others were at a loss as to how to respond, and the Queen relaxed back, satisfied, into her thick, red couch.

"*Enough* of this prattle." She waved her hand. "Our forces are set to wage battle at dawn, and *we* must have our beauty sleep. You are dismissed."

Lee wasn't sure what she meant by that. She tried to decipher the Queen's glare, unsuccessfully. "So... we can go now? We're free?"

"Don't be ridiculous," the Queen said, flatly. "*Of course* not. Report to the officers at once. Have them outfit you with armor and weaponry and assign you to your positions. *Chop-chop!*" She clapped her fat hands twice, her rings making sharp clangs.

"She will do no such thing!" Percy drew his brow into an angry wrinkle. "To conscript us four to this mad crusade of yours is one thing, but you leave the girl out of it."

Óseo stepped up to Percy's right, looking as menacing as a skeleton could. The Queen was stunned—it was clear she was unaccustomed to such blatant defiance. Then she smiled, the way a cobra smiles. She pursed her little mouth and gave a sharp whistle, which brought her guards into the tent.

"It's okay." Lee turned to her friends. "We'll figure it out." She wasn't sure that they would, but getting into trouble now would not help find her father. The guards escorted them out the tent. The Queen looked at Lee, triumphant. Lee looked back, unimpressed.

A few of the guards took them over to another tent, full of equipment, to receive theirs. They were handed round helmets, which were too big for Lee's and Óseo's heads and too small to fit on top of Madame Couronne's jar, and five vests, two made of rigid fabric filled with something hard, two made of bamboo canes, and one made of dark green tweed. They were each given a weapon: Percy and Óseo received rusty muskets, though, as new recruits, they weren't entitled to ammunition yet. Mrs. Adocchiare was handed a scimitar. Madame Couronne, a longbow and a large belt quiver with six arrows, three of which were missing at least one row of feathers. And Lee received a heavy mace with metal bulges that were dented in with use. Afterward, they were discharged for the rest of the night, to prepare for combat at daybreak.

Their tent was small and had one electric lantern hanging at its center and nothing else. They dropped their equipment in a pile and sat on the ground, disheartened.

"Oh, dear, it seems we're in a bit of a pickle." Mrs. Adocchiare tried her best not to sound too gloomy. "The people here… it's so sad when people of faith lose their way. I wouldn't want to offend their beliefs, of course, but…." She paused apologetically.

"Idiots *ought* to be offended!" Madame Couronne exclaimed. "Respect for everyone's world view, in ze end, it leads to intellectual paralysis. You spend so much time respecting zat you haven't time left to zink."

"Sí," Óseo agreed. "The royal gasbag, she is completamente loca. La tengo por imposible."

"Oh, but please don't let that dreadful Queen make you think badly of spirituality. It really is a most wonderful thing," Mrs. Adocchiare implored.

Percy shook his head. "I have no quarrel with spirituality. But I find that religion is an enlightened, intelligent thing suffering a benighted, unintelligent following."

Lee thought it over and concluded that it was a subject best left to think about another time.

"Besides," Óseo continued, "I du not want tu be in any army that actually wants me in it. Je je je je je!" He winked at Lee. He pushed his straw hat back on his head and scratched his skull, producing a sound a little like a metal pan being scrubbed, and looked at the others. "I have a plan."

They leaned in to listen.

"We split up and look for Lee's father around the camp. We've seen his portrait twice now, so we should recognize him no problem. If we find him—tumorrow, when the fighting starts, we escape tugether in all the confusion. And if we du not find him here, we use the chaos tu go look in the King's army. ¿What du yu say, niña?"

Niña liked the idea. So did the rest.

"Hear, hear." Percy smiled with both mouth and mustache. "Good work, old boy!" He gave Óseo a hearty pat on the back, popping out his collarbone, which Óseo caught midair. "Well, let's not dilly-dally. Time's short and work's aplenty, so let's get to it, shall we? Lee, dear, you best not wander these grounds by your lonesome. Come with me."

They split up, each choosing a section of the camp to cover. Lee set off alongside Percy, scouring the area near the gate. They skulked between the raggedy tents, carefully peeking into each, met only by sad, downtrodden faces, covered in layers of armor and weaponry and grime. The Queen's glorious army.

Eventually, they ran out of tents to check, so they headed back. Lee didn't hold out hope that any of the others had found her father, and their apologetic looks as she entered the tent confirmed it. If she were to find her father in Nowhere, it would not be in Eponymia. She flopped down on the ground, closed her eyes, and prepared for war.

VIII

The pale sky seemed to signal more the death of night than the birth of day. The sunless dawn was already tired with what was to come.

Lee hadn't slept a wink. She was tired. She was worried about her father, and about her mother being worried about her. And she was afraid, down to the pit of her stomach. She desperately wished they were there to protect her.

She laid there, looking out the tent at the few shapes that moved about the camp, when a loud bugle sounded.

People scurried out of their tents, men and women and children armed with a variety of weapons—some familiar, others unusual and bizarre, and most obsolete. They hurried to form long rows of three in front of the camp, with officers in flamboyant uniforms of gold, silver, and royal blue heading each row. Lee noticed they were the only soldiers in the Queen's entire army to have uniforms. It didn't seem very practical.

After putting on their armor and weapons, to varying degrees of success, Lee and the others joined the rest of the army already assembled. They hurried to the back without anyone noticing and slipped into place. A few orders were being barked at the troops by the officers up front, but Lee was too far away and too short and too anxious to hear them. It was an army of hundreds, maybe more, Lee wasn't sure. The rows started moving, in synch, no one uttering as much as a syllable.

As they marched onward, the day got brighter and hotter. Mrs. Adocchiare tried to wear her helmet and hard vest and carry her sword without complaining, but Madame Couronne, having failed to fit her helmet either on or into her jar, discreetly threw it behind some black bushes, though she kept her bow and arrows. Percy hung his musket off his shoulder and fastened his helmet under his chin. He was the only one of them that looked anything like a real soldier. Óseo tried to do the same, but his musket strap and bamboo vest kept sliding off, so he carried them instead, and managed to get his saucer-shaped helmet to stay on by wearing it on top of his hat. Lee's green felt vest and bowl helmet fit well enough, and her side bag was much lighter, now that she'd eaten half the apples in it, but her mace eventually became too heavy to hold up, even with two hands, so she held it by the strap of its handle and dragged it behind her on the ground. No doubt, they were the sorriest-looking bunch in a sorry-looking army.

Lee had been expecting a long march, but to her surprise they were ordered to stop and assume battle formations by the early afternoon. The three long rows split up into dozens of shorter rows of three, spreading themselves across the shoulder of a wide U-shaped valley. Lee, Óseo, Percy, Madame Couronne, and Mrs. Adocchiare stood side by side, each as the last in a row, and looked around worriedly, not knowing what to expect. The valley was still, bathed in muddy light, but it slowly filled with the muffled echoing of something approaching.

"¡There!" said Óseo.

Lee followed his stare to the opposite shoulder across the valley and a long fence of people—enemy soldiers. They were too far away to see clearly, but she got the impression they were just as much of a miserable, ragtag army, if somewhat smaller.

The two armies stood there, facing each other across the yawn of the valley, neither making the first move. Percy looked alert, like he was expecting something else, like when one sees a flash of lightening and waits ready for the boom of thunder. Suddenly, a low, deep growl resonated throughout the valley, bouncing back and forth between the slopes. Behind the line of the King's men, a row of big machine rigs emerged—catapults, carrying immense boulders.

"Dear me!" Mrs. Adocchiare gasped.

The fear that had earlier nestled in Lee's stomach was now at her throat. Her breathing became shallow and fast.

"I cannot remember the last time I felt my heart beat in my chest," Óseo said, dealing with things his usual way, "but if I still had a heart, it would be beating like a bongo drum."

"Now, now—we must keep our wits about us," Percy called them to order. "War is a competition of mistakes, with victory to he who makes the least. We must remain vigilant for the most opportune time to make our escape. Do not let yourself be gripped in histrionics."

No sooner did he finish than a sharp, arched whistle cut through the air, and a rock the size of a car slammed into the Queen's forces not thirty yards away from them. Soldiers went flying through the air and falling into the valley below. Another whistle followed, and another torrent of dirt and people flew overhead and down the slope. The Queen's officers shouted attack orders, and the army, with Lee and the others in tow, rushed down toward the King's army. The Queen's soldiers clashed into the King's like pounding surf into hard sand. Men, woman, even children threw themselves into violent mayhem.

"Come—we must flee now!" Percy shouted. They broke from the crowd, circumventing clusters of battling soldiers, avoiding as much of the fighting as they could. Rocks kept hailing down around them, filling the air with whistles and smashing soldiers and machinery indiscriminately. People shouted and screamed. They could feel pain, Lee realized, but, being dead, they simply rose back up to keep fighting, without end. She understood then—if she got hurt, if she died there, she could never go back.

She ran across the battlefield, behind Percy and Óseo and ahead of Mrs. Adocchiare and Madame Couronne; she ran as swiftly and as nimbly as she could, until her side hurt and her thighs felt like heavy sacks of water. But she didn't slow down—she didn't dare. She hurdled wreckage and rocks and holes in the ground until something grabbed her by the leg, sending her mace flying and making her fall flat on her face into the dirt. Her head banged hard against the inside of her helmet like a bell clapper. She looked up to see her canvases and brushes scattered. Behind her, a man, half-buried in the earth with his arm and part of his head jutting out, held onto her. His grip was unrelenting. The soil filled his open mouth, preventing him from making a sound, but his uncovered eye locked with Lee's, mocking her as she tried to wiggle free. She screamed loud enough to bring the others rushing back. Without slowing down, Madame Couronne lifted up her dress and kicked the man's arm, snapping it off like a twig and sending it flipping through the air. Long, pink worms came writhing out the stump of his shoulder. Lee quickly picked herself up, collected her art supplies, and resumed running.

They ran even faster, crossing deeper and deeper into the King's army's territory. Most of the King's soldiers charged past them, though some did notice them and attacked. They managed to narrowly escape one squad of soldiers just as a giant boulder landed on top of them. Percy and Óseo used their muskets as clubs, swinging at attackers as they ran past, in one case knocking a head clean off a soldier's shoulders. Mrs. Adocchiare swung her scimitar up to deflect the blow from a man with a horned helmet, and, while clumsily swiveling it around, knocked down three others. Madame Couronne, covering Lee's back, faced a woman the size of a refrigerator wearing a shirt of metal scales and a long fur dress and waving something that looked like a giant boomerang made of massive fangs. The woman threw herself screaming at Madame Couronne, who calmly plucked Lee's helmet off her head and bashed it into the woman's face, sending her spinning like a top and crashing into the soldiers behind her.

Their break away from the troops was successful, if somewhat ungraceful, and they reached the bottom of the shoulder rim, under the line of catapults. Lee had a chance to catch her breath and to grasp just how horrible it all was. She was scared, but also angry—at being scared, and at the soldiers, and the King and Queen for making her scared.

"O, what men dare do!" Percy shook his stretched-down mustache.

"Zese vulgarians," Madame Couronne said, nodding back, "all zis chaos and ridiculous warfare—it simply goes to show zat intelligent people do zings intelligently, while unintelligent people do zings, well…"

They climbed up the slope and reached the giant rigs, which were being loaded and launched in turns.

"Hey! What youse doin' here? You ain't nonea us!" A child, possibly a couple of years younger than Lee, with a pointy helmet and dark brown freckles covering his cheeks, ran toward them. Others came running to his side, and in an instant Lee and her friends were surrounded by a large half-circle of child soldiers.

"Amigos…" Óseo spread out his skeletal hands, smiling. "We are not the enemy. We are just looking for someone. Yu du not want tu hurt us—we can see that yu are very busy. Yu should let us go, and we will bother yu no longer, eh?"

They looked at each other, then at Lee and her friends—their helmets, vests, weapons, dirty faces, and ruffled clothing—then at each other again, then pointed all their gun barrels and blades at them.

"This is not good," Óseo whispered. "These mocosos are tu eager; they will not listen tu reason."

The boy soldiers slowly started advancing. Lee inched backwards with the others, looking over her shoulder; behind them was a catapult, and beyond that the deep valley. There was no escape. She looked around urgently.

"The catapult," she cried. "Let's get on the catapult!"

The others followed her onto the machine. Óseo and Percy pushed the thing until its four big wheels started turning and it groaned in protest toward the edge of the slope.

The soldiers rushed them, throwing things and shooting at them, filling the air with puffs of splinters and sawdust and the shrilling sounds of bullets burrowing into timber. The front wheels went over the flat end, and Lee could feel the machine beginning to tilt. She was afraid of the drop, but the whizzing bullets around her terrified her even more.

Percy and Óseo jumped on the back ramp just as the catapult flew downhill. Percy quickly ducked behind one of the rear beams, the bullets missing his head by inches, but Óseo got hit by a large steel pellet right in the center of his back, shattering him to pieces. Luckily for him his clothes kept most of his bones together, and Percy and Mrs. Adocchiare and Madame Couronne hurried to grab his other pieces before they fell through the catapult's undercarriage. His head, however, rolled past them and fell to the ground, tumbling downhill alongside them, gathering momentum. Without thinking, Lee swung off the side holding on with one hand, her head dangling a couple of feet above the speeding ground, and caught the skull just before it rolled out of reach.

"¡Muchas gracias, chica! I know I shouldn't lose my head, je je je je je."

Even though she was hanging off a plummeting catapult, she giggled a "you're welcome." Madame Couronne, finding the time to grudge in French, tossed her bow, emptied her quiver of its six arrows, and poured Óseo into it, placing his head on top. He seemed more than willing to endure his accommodations, seeing how much it annoyed Madame Couronne to carry him.

"Now, this is what yu call dead weight, sí? ¡Je je je je je!"

"Be quiet, you pile of dominoes." Madame Couronne scowled.

The catapult reached the bottom of the slope, its momentum carrying it forward onto the plain. It bumped and skipped over rocks and debris, its wheels

wobbling around their axes as they pulverized whatever came under them. Raggedy and falling apart, it finally swerved to a stop. There was no fighting in their immediate vicinity, and they took a collective breath. They were safe, at least for now.

"Bien," Óseo said from his quiver, "looks like we all made it out in one piece. Well, except for me, of course."

Mrs. Adocchiare looked dazed, like she was searching for a fitting expression. Her windswept cotton-candy hair was the now the shape of a cone. Percy and Lee exchanged smiles.

Suddenly, a tattooed man swinging a giant axe jumped out at them from behind the machine. The thought that it was too late to react flashed through Lee's mind, when the catapult's arm sprang from the tattered ropes holding it down and knocked the man square in the chin, sending him spinning through the air in an arc of flailing and squealing with a reverberating *spraaangggggggggggggggggggg.*

They stumbled off the machine and looked around. The direction to the King's camp was easy to determine, based on the catapults' wheel marks they'd spotted on top. They climbed up the valley away from the battle and followed that direction, into the land of Shibbolet.

IX

The King's base was closer to the valley than the Queen's. They reached it in no time at all. Smaller and more sophisticated, it was a different type of camp. It was surrounded by two protective mounds, a tall one and around it a shorter one. Each had a gate, made of two rows of sharpened wood columns; one row stood upright while the other projected diagonally out from between, like clasped fingers.

The four of them tiptoed closer, finding cover behind the perimeter mound.

"Wait," Percy said, shaking his finger. "We best not be found out." He tilted his head in the direction of the gate not far down, where two guards stood.

"Sí, we du not want tu be captured again," Óseo said, looking around from the quiver by Madame Couronne's side.

Mrs. Adocchiare, who stood next to Lee, reached for the left side of her face and plucked out her eye with a soggy "*POP*." "This should do it," she held out her open palm, presenting her eye in a tiny pink puddle.

She smiled with a dark, gaping socket hole above her plump cheek.

"Très bien." Madame Couronne gave a nod of approval.

Mrs. Adocchiare held up her eye above the mound and slowly swiveled it around, like a submarine periscope. "Providence shines on us—the guards have their backs to us. We should hurry." She turned her other eye, the one still in her head, to Percy.

On his signal, they all climbed over the mound and hurried to hide behind the next one. Up close, it was significantly taller than the first, over twice as tall, and lacked enough ridges and bumps for Lee to get a foothold. Mrs. Adocchiare tried but failed to reach the rim to look around.

"Humph," Percy humphed. "Very well. Up you go then." He kneeled down, but Mrs. Adocchiare wasn't sure what he meant.

"Climb onto my shoulders, woman. Hurry up, we haven't got all day!"

"Oh!" She placed one foot on his bent thigh, the other on his shoulder, then, supporting herself against the mound, stood up on shaky legs. With a deep groan, Percy rose to his feet, pushing Mrs. Adocchiare up to the edge of the mound. She was a small woman, but then again, he was a small man.

She carefully surveyed the area as Percy wobbled under her. Lee found the whole thing very comical, but Mrs. Adocchiare was able to get a good look. "Thank goodness, they're still busy doing whatever it is they're doing. They're paying no attention to this direction."

With a few quick exchanges, Percy pushed her feet up and helped her on top of the mound, then did the same for Madame Couronne and Óseo, rattling around in her quiver, and then for Lee, who in turn helped Madame Couronne pull Percy up. They all made the jump down the other side safely and rushed to the rear of a nearby hut.

The inside of the camp consisted of two long rows of large, rectangular huts facing each other, and one square hut in the middle at the far end, facing the camp gates. The camp appeared to be empty, save for the guards and six or seven soldiers stationed outside the square hut. That's where they'd find the King, Lee bet.

They crept across the camp, from hut to hut, until they reached the end of the barracks, across from the King's cabin. Now all that stood in their way was the King's personal guard.

Lee mulled over their options: one, storm the place—but they'd all left their armor and weapons behind, and besides, they wouldn't stand a chance anyway; two, bypass the guards—but the guards completely surrounded the King's quarters; and three—their final option—create a diversion and sneak in when the guards weren't looking. A solid enough plan, if she could come up with the right distraction.

"I'll be right back."

She took Óseo's head out and rummaged through the quiver until she found one of his hands. She took it and, despite her friends' hushed protests, slinked into the cabin they were hiding behind. A moment later she came out the front entrance, wearing bulky, adult-size armor that she'd found inside, and walked straight up to the guards.

"Hey!" she called out in her deepest voice, bunching up her face to look as tough as possible. "I saw enemy soldiers hiding by the gate. They looked very dangerous—one was a mean skeleton. And the guards over there aren't even looking." She pointed at them with Óseo's hand, which she held out of her stretched pajama sleeve as if it was her own. Óseo pointed his finger at the gate. She suddenly realized she was holding it in the wrong hand, with its fingers facing out, and hurried to put it down.

The guards all ran to the gate.

"Don't worry, I'll stay here and keep an eye out," she cried after them, but they didn't seem to care. She nodded toward her friends, who came quickly out of their hiding place, and together the five of them entered the King's cabin.

The cabin consisted of two large rooms, divided by a solid wood wall with an open doorway in the middle. Strange-looking maps covered the walls of the first room, with a large table filled with sand, shaped to look like the valley and the area around it, at its center.

They entered the second room, which was smaller but more elegant. The floor was covered by a wine-colored carpet, and a long darkwood table surrounded by thick leather chairs stood at its rear. As soon as Lee walked in, she was greeted by a terrible, bitter acid stench that burned her throat and eyes and filled her lungs, making it hard to breathe. A thick soup of smoke swirled about the room. It concentrated at the far end of the table, where a short, bald man was sitting behind a small, green glass lamp, pouring over some maps and charts. The light from the lamp reflected in his circle-rimmed glasses, making him appear as if he had headlights for eyes. He wore a dark robe, and on top of it, thrown casually around his shoulders, a large coat made of rough hides, big-cat pelts with spots and stripes, and a tuft of small black and white feathers around the collar. He was too absorbed in his work to notice them until they were practically on top of him.

"WHAt is THe meaning of THis? HOw did you get in HEre witHOUt summons? Are you... are you asSAssins?" A waft of dark smoke escaped his mouth with each vowel: WHAt—*puff*...THe—*puff*...THis—*puff*...HOw—*puff*...HEre—*puff*...withHOUt—*puff*....

"We are not indeed, sir." Percy tried to calm him.

"Spies?"

"Upon my word we are not, sir," Percy insisted. "We are in need of your aid."

The man looked back suspiciously, examining the group up and down and up again. Lee realized how she must look and quickly shed her heavy armor to the floor, handing Óseo's hand back to Madame Couronne. She smiled at the man. His skin reminded her of books left in storefront windows by the end of summer.

"Indeed? HOw so?" he said, rebalancing the glasses on the bridge of his nose. Another smoggy vapor puffed out his mouth and drifted upwards. His cause of death was pretty clear.

"I'm looking for my father," Lee said directly. "We were in Eponymia, and the Queen made us be in her army, but my dad wasn't there, so we ran away when the fighting started and came here. Ca—may we look to see if he's in your army, please, sir?"

"*Your MAjesty*," he corrected her, humorlessly. "THere is pROtocol to be FOllowed." He rose from behind the long table, fastening the skins and furs around him. "COme. WAlk with me."

They exited the cabin just as the guards returned from their futile search. The King dismissed them.

"Our HIstory HEre, as much as anyone HAs committed to memory, HAs been a bloody moSAic of WAr between THe kingdoms." He walked them down the path between the cabins, his personal guard following from a distance. He strode with his hands held behind his back, leaving in his wake little billows of smoke for Lee to dodge. "On THe OTHer side of THe valley is THe kingdom of Eponymia. Eponymians are rabid zealots, HAnging on THe Queen's every word in THeir blind worship of THe great adversary."

"You mean Ovo?" Óseo said. The King looked around until he found the source of the question. He nodded, as if he was well accustomed to skulls talking out of quivers.

"THey HAve perverted our sacred and riGHteous ovO into Ovo—a blasPHEmous distortion!" An angry dark cloud *puff*ed out his mouth, leaving a lingering trail.

"But I still don't understand, what's the big difference?" asked Lee.

The King stared at her blankly.

"WHy, it's THe biggest difference THat can exist. It's THe diametrically-opposed, eXAct opposite. If ovO is all THat is good, THen HIs reverse—Ovo—by definition is all THat is bad! Every CHild in SHibbolet knows this." *Puff—puff—puff—puff—puff—puff— puff—puff—puff—puff—puff.*

"But it's still the same name. It's exactly the same both ways! There's a word for that…" She couldn't quite remember what it was.

"THat is quite beside THe point." The King held up his ash-yellow hand to silence her. "We are not faNAtics like our ENemy; we are a REasonable and civilized people. We ONly—"

"Palindrome!" Lee jumped, remembering. "It's called a palindrome, when you can read a word from both directions the same way."

The King gave an empty response, his face carved from stiff wood. They had reached the end of the path. He turned around. "Ours is a HOly war. We fIGHt it not because we CHOOse to, but because we MUst."

"But you're the King. Can't you just decide you don't want to fight anymore?"

"I am but a HUmble servant of my people. It is my obliGAtion to follow THeir will."

"But I thought you also tell them what to do? Then who makes all the decisions?" She was confused.

"I'm afraid it's not quite THat simple," he said, giving the same answer adults always give when they're asked a question they prefer not to answer. Seemed simple enough to Lee. The King made decisions based on what his subjects wanted, and they had to obey his orders, so that way nobody really had to be responsible for anything. The Queen may have been giddy with war, but at least she was honest about it.

"You MUst undersTAnd; we are simply proTEcting THe sanctity of ovO."

"Perhaps we invented gods so we can put ze blame on zem, non?" Madame Couronne said with admirably well-concealed ridicule.

"So," Lee said, quickly changing the subject, "can we please find out if my father is in your army, Your Majesty? I'm really afraid he'll get hurt. I want to take him home."

"SUch FOrtitude for SUch a little girl. I'm impREessed." The King looked at her with his sphinx expression. "And WHere mIGHt HOme be?"

She thought about the best answer to give. "I'm not from around here."

"AHh!" A big, heavy *puff* escaped him. "An OUtlander." He walked on, hands still clasped behind his back. "Our army is sMAll. We HAven't HAd new recruits in a VEry, VEry long time, MUch longer THan before you were born, I'm sure. So WHerever your FAther is, it's not HEre."

She nodded at the ground. Each time she failed to find him, it was like a small piece of his memory faded away.

"But I'm SUre we can find a place for THe five of you in our RAnks—you're clearly a BOld and reSOurceful BUnch. You'll MAke fine soldiers." The King clenched the borders of his coat. "CAptains, even!"

"We are humbled by your praise, Your Majesty. But I'm afraid we must decline," Percy replied. "And we best be on our way—nightfall approaches."

The King stopped. They were back where they had started, in front of his cabin. He turned to face them. He pushed his glasses up his nose, collecting himself, and smirked.

"I'm afraid I CAn't let you do THat. Our army is underMAnned as it is—we simply CAnnot forgo five prime recruits SUch as YOurselves. Well," he said, looking at Óseo, "fOur, anyway. I'm SOrry, but it REally is out of my HAnds—it's THe law. MAndatory conscriptIOn and all THat. I'm SUre you undersTAnd." He headed back to his cabin, waving his guards to take them away.

"Nom d'un chien!" Madame Couronne called out.

"What is the meaning of this? Are you bloody daft, man?" Percy yelled furiously, but the King had already disappeared into his quarters, leaving a foul trail of smoke behind.

There was no point trying to resist the guards. They were taken to one of the huts at the front of the camp. The space was filled with bunk beds and smelled of rust and rot. The walls were dirt-discolored, the ceiling blackened with smudges of something that had once been wet and was now powdery. They flopped down on the bottom bunk beds, not saying a word. Even Percy's mustache drooped. Lee put aside her bag, took Madame Couronne's quiver, poured Óseo onto the bed, and the two of them started putting him back together.

"Well, zis is certainly a new nadir for us. If it's not one zing, it's ze ozer." Her groan turned into a grunt.

"Oh, stuff and nonsense," Mrs. Adocchiare said, keeping her smile up. "It'll all turn out for the best, you'll see."

"No, it won't." Lee said, connecting Óseo's parts. "I'm sorry. I'm sorry I dragged you all into this. It's all my fault."

"Oh, pshaw!" Percy's mustache snapped back into shape. "Take heart, dear child—why, if not for you, we'd still be trapped in that room, twiddling our thumbs 'til time everlasting. For all our troubles since, we seem to be none the worse for the wear, and it's been a jolly good romp, eh?"

Lee nodded, indifferent. She handed a few ribs from her side of the pile to Madame Couronne, who was working on Óseo's ribcage. She smiled back through her dirty jar. "Mais certainement."

"¡Seguro!" Óseo agreed, giggling—Madame Couronne's handling of his ribs tickled him. "I know it's been a long journey, chica, and things look bleak now, but yu will find yur father—I promise yu this."

"How would *you* know?" Lee said, more than a little insolent.

With the exception of some small bones still on the bed, Óseo was pretty much put together, and he sat up to button his silky blue shirt. He took his straw hat, flipped it in his bony hand, and placed it on Lee's head with a smile, pulling it down over her eyes. She had no choice but to let a little smile escape.

"Because yu are yu."

"Indeed, in all this hubbub, we've hardly had a chance to reflect," Percy said. "We've looked for your father everywhere in Nowhere, which was not such a big place, and couldn't find him anywhere. Now we are in Elsewhere, which, it seems, is much larger, but we at least know that he must be here, somewhere. All that remains to be determined, therefore," he reasoned, "is exactly where."

"¡El bigote is right, niña!" Óseo jumped off the bed, good as new. "Las parcas, the three old sisters, they told us tu go past the warzone. We should look tu see if he's there."

"But how? We're trapped here now," Lee moaned.

"Don't worry niña—in a battle of wits, we are better armed than both these armies, sí?"

She didn't follow.

"¿We escaped from one, sí?"

"Um, sí...." she answered, tentatively.

"¿And we broke intu the other, sí?"

"Sí."

"Then it shoud not be tu hard tu du it again, sí?"

"¡Sí!"

"¡Je je je je je!" He was pleased.

"I concur," Percy concurred, which Lee assumed meant he agreed. "For the nonce, we are in no immediate peril. But we must plan our escape without delay. I, for one, have had quite enough of this land steeped in madness."

"Oh, we shouldn't judge the Shibboletanians and Eponymians too harshly, just because of those two scoundrels who rule over them. I'm sure they're all very nice people at heart." Mrs. Adocchiare stayed positive. Lee wondered if she agreed.

"Mon dieu!" Madame Couronne shook her shoulders so that her head shook in her jar. "People get ze goverment zey deserve. Zese people have been fighting for an eternity over ze pronunciation of a name. Obviously, zere is not an intelligent one among zem—and if you're not as intelligent as you can be, well, zen, to hell wiz you!"

"But can't we make them see?" said Lee. "If we just help them—"

"'*If* zis and *if* zat—my mozer used to say zat '*if*' and hot water do not a soup make. I cannot but conclude ze bulk of ze natives here to be ze most pernicious race of little odious vermin."

Lee didn't know what to say in return.

"Yu don't really like people, du yu, Señora Coron?" Óseo giggled.

"Pffah!" She scoffed with a haughty tilt of her head, brought about with a shrug. "Hell is ozer people."

"So you think they'll all just go on and on fighting forever?" Lee addressed no one in particular.

"I do not know. I sincerely hope not," Percy answered while concentrating on brushing off his outfit with a rag he'd found. "Both people, each in their own way, sincerely believe in the indisputable righteousness of their cause. Each believes, wholeheartedly and without reserve, that they are on the side of good. And people, I've come to learn, are at their most dangerous when they are convinced of their righteousness."

She nodded. She knew most people weren't really bad: bad things happen when people think they have the right to do what they're doing instead of the responsibility to not do it.

"But you need not worry yourself about such matters, dear. It's late, and we face a testing day tomorrow. I suggest you rest and gather your strength," Percy said.

She agreed and found herself yawning loudly. She lay down where she sat, resting her head in the lap of Mrs. Adocchiare. The old woman gave off warmth like a radiator. She drifted into sleep and dreamed of her family.

X

Lee woke up, gradually, and blinked and stretched her way to standing. The others were already up, nervously walking around the large hut, tinkering with the different artifacts scattered about, mostly pieces of weapons and armor. She looked out the barred row of windows; the sky was a great violet. Another battle was only hours away, and the odds were stacked against them.

Mrs. Adocchiare assisted Percy in laying out the arsenal on their beds. Lee picked out a long chainmail shirt, like a knight's, which almost reached her feet. It was terribly heavy, but after the last battle, she wanted the protection. She took a belt, which was too big to buckle, and tied it around her waist, making a dress of the shirt. The helmet was more modern, a half-shell with a narrow visor on the front. She guessed it used to be a motorcycle helmet. Instead of an offensive weapon, Percy equipped her with a long triangular shield.

Óseo found a mostly complete, if scraped and dented, suit of ancient Roman armor. Lee's favorite part was the helmet, like a bronze bucket with a fin of hair on top that looked like a broom. "Broomtop!" She snickered, pointing, but he didn't seem to mind. Percy and Mrs. Adocchiare limited themselves to just helmets, favoring lightness over protection, while Madame Couronne didn't even bother with that.

"Hey, you!" A grimy soldier, whose few bottom teeth covered his upper lip, rattled a sledgehammer across the window bars. "Get ready. We head out in five."

Lee made sure her chainmail dress was well fastened, and that everything was in her side bag: the paint tubes and brushes and palette and canvases, now dirtied, and the few apples she had left. She hadn't eaten since yesterday, she realized, or drank for that matter, but she didn't feel hungry or thirsty. Things worked differently there, though the idea that she didn't need food or drink to stay alive was disturbing. She ate an apple, just in case.

"Now," Percy said, "remain close together. We must be ready for the most favourable chance to abscond, and promptly concoct a way by which to do so. We are all in agreement, I take it?"

They were. But this time, when the King's army mobilized, they found themselves marched to the front. Their battalion didn't consist of that many troops—a couple of hundred at most, Lee guessed—and had no catapults or any other great machines of destruction accompanying it. Most of the weapons she scouted were blades or blunt instruments, with only a few bows and guns, which she found to be half a comfort. The thought of another battle filled her with dread.

They walked in the general direction of Eponymia but didn't follow the deep wheel tracks to the valley. Their path took them more to the right, toward a hill range the color of copper. The land was quiet—quiet enough to hear the rustle of pebbles underfoot and the occasional gust of wind. The only exception to the silence was a low mechanical hum, which emanated from somewhere behind them, maintaining a feeling of unease.

About an hour or so into their march, they arrived at another battlefield. The battle that took place there was recent, probably during the night, Lee assumed, by the still-smoldering ashes scattered about, though there were no people there. A few skeletal vultures circled above, flapping their enormous wings. At the orders of someone at the back, they stopped. She turned around to see if she could see what was making the mechanical grumble. The King himself was there, riding in a fancy old car, the kind with no roof and with big brass pipes coming out the sides, driven by one of his guards. Except the guard wasn't actually driving the thing; the running engine was what generated the noise, probably for effect, but the car was carried by sixteen large men, four in the front and four in the back on each side, shouldering two very long metal poles fastened to it.

A growing clamor from the opposing hilltops got Lee's attention, and all at once she was on the brink of panic—the Eponymian forces came spilling over. They greatly outnumbered the Shibboletanians, and the terrain didn't seem wide enough to allow her and the others easy escape. A round shape slowly rose between the hills ahead. It grew as big as an elephant, covered in strips of lilac and royal blue and lime green and corn yellow fabrics, adorned with a glittering ring of gold and silver fringes around its circumference. It was the Queen, sitting in a giant wicker chair carried by a group of guards.

Swaying as her porters brought her to a stop, the Queen exchanged scornful glares with the King, who humphed back, releasing a small puff of smoke from the corner of his mouth. She then spotted Lee and the others. Her nostrils flared. Her little downturned mouth arched even more, into a perfect upside-down U. Her entire enormous mass heaved with fury. Lee realized that was exactly why the King placed them at the head of his army.

The two armies faced each other.

"Cabezas de calabazas," Óseo said, clucking his tongue and shaking his big red fin. "They intend tu fight simply by throwing themselves at each other."

Percy sighed, drawing his great white eyebrows together. "This does not bode well. We are between hammer and anvil."

The King and Queen locked gazes across the hills. Everyone held their breath. Without taking his eyes off the Queen, the King gave a slight bob of his head, signaling his driver to slam his hand on the horn, producing a long, piercing noise.

The soldiers started running toward each other, and Lee and the others were swept up in the surge of men and women shouting and screaming and waving weapons. A colossus of a man, with chains crossing his chest and a helmet with long spikes, was the first to attack them, wielding a long broadsword in each hand. He slammed into Lee's shield with a loud *clang*, pushing her knees to the ground. She screamed. He laid down another powerful blow to the shield, rattling all her joints. Percy and Óseo flanked him, assaulting him with their weapons, Óseo with a short sword and Percy with a musket with a bayonet at its end, but the giant man managed to repel them, landing yet a third and a forth blow to her shield. The last one bent the shield and crushed her completely into the ground, fracturing the dry earth around her.

She screamed at the top of her lungs, and her mouth filled with dirt. She closed her eyes, bracing for the final blow, but instead she was yanked out from under the shield by Mrs. Adocchiare and Madame Couronne, each grabbing on to an arm, just as the man collapsed the shield like so much cardboard. They wasted no time: Percy jumped on the giant's back and grabbed his arms. Óseo, Mrs. Adocchiare, and Madame Couronne together went to work on his head, mercilessly kicking and punching and hitting him with all their might, until he finally fell to the ground, defeated.

Lee's back and arms throbbed with pain, but nothing felt broken. There was no time to catch her breath—others were heading toward them. They ran, Óseo holding on to her with his bony hand. She could see the Queen's shape swaying wildly, and on the opposite hill the King's chimney of smoke puffs, both barking orders at their captains.

They darted amidst the fighting, mostly forward, sometimes sideways or backwards, but time and again failed to make their way outwards and to safety. They tried for an opening in the pandemonium, when a tall man with a whip and a shorter man with a revolver and a monkey on his shoulder closed them off completely. Lee was the first to recognize them. "Sõt! Ringmaster Phineas!"

The two men stopped.

"Lee!" The taller man took off his helmet, revealing Ringmaster Phineas's smiling face. "Look, Sõt, it's pretty princess Lee. And her cordial crew of caring cohorts."

"'allo." Sõt nodded politely. "You remember Sulyok, right?"

At the mention of his name, the pointy-eared monkey turned his head toward Lee and hissed.

"Friends! What a fine fluke that we have found ourselves facing each other in the field of battle. I figure you, like us, have failed to flee the fiendish forces of the monarchs, and are forced to fight, eh?"

"Sí." Óseo nodded his red fin.

"We're trying to escape," Mrs. Adocchiare explained.

"I don't think you can," said Sõt, glancing around. "It's too crowded here. We're like monkeys in a barrel."

"Mon dieu! Again wiz ze monkeys. We are not monkeys, you oaf. I used to be seventh in succession to ze crown of France!"

Sulyok responded with a "*hisssssssssssss!*"

"Nevertheless," said Percy, "even though we seem to have found a short respite, we are still in midst of battle, and I fail to see how we might escape it—we are surrounded on all sides."

Lee looked at the King and Queen perched on their respective hilltops, watching the battle as if it were a show put on for their behalf. This gave her an idea.

"Ringmaster Phineas...." He bent down, and she whispered in his ear. He straightened up, all excited and raring to go.

"Marvelous! A magnificently masterful plan."

The others looked at them for explanation, but Lee just pointed to a hilltop not far off, opposite the ones the royals occupied. She sprinted alongside Phineas toward it, the others following closely. She was the first to reach it, Madame Couronne the last.

Ringmaster Phineas took a quick moment to catch his breath, then sucked in as much air as he could before releasing it: "*Laaaadies and gentlemeeeen! Children of aaaall ages!*" His voice was big and booming, bouncing between the hills like a pinball. "*It is my pleasure and privilege to present to you people, with great pride and prestige, and to proclaim with profuse praise and pomp, the most paramount of popular performers, a positively precious and perfectly powerful pontificator, of prime probity and purity, and accompanied by her prized party of peers...without further ado, I give you...the one...the only...Leeeeeeeee!*"

He had certainly managed to grab everyone's attention. All the fighting stopped, and all eyes were fixed upon Lee, including the King's and Queen's.

She stepped forward, mustering the courage to speak. "Hello." There were hundreds of them, waiting to hear what she had to say. She knew that nearly as important as what she was about to say was how she was going to say it. She cleared her throat.

"I'm Lee. I'm not from around here. I actually came here from pretty far away."

"Outlander," the word repeated in loud whispers throughout the crowd.

"And, um, sometimes... sometimes we don't really notice what we're doing, we don't realize it, until somebody else, who can see us from the outside, points it out to us, and they make us realize it. You know what I mean?"

"No!" A man shouted, even though the question was rhetorical.

"Since I arrived here, in Elsewhere, I've travelled a lot. Me and my friends, we've walked through Eponymia and Shibbolet—we're looking for my father. I haven't found him, yet. But... but what I did find was a lot of destruction. Everywhere we went and everywhere I looked, everything was broken. And I went through an entire town that's deserted because everyone's here, fighting. I met people who had to hide in the forest because they didn't want to fight in this war. And..." She searched for the rest of the thought. "It's heartbreaking. Really. It's so sad that even when you're dead, you have to fight all the time. Why—"

"It is the will of *Ovo!*" The Queen shouted from her hilltop, wobbling her large basket chair atop her struggling bearers. "The little girl is just a *little girl*— what does *she* know? She doesn't have any *idea* what she's talking about. We fight for the *glory* of Ovo, the *almighty!*"

"BAh!" Dark smoke billowed from the King. "Your 'Ovo' is a FArce! It's ovO THat is gLOrious and almIGHty. It's ovO THat's THe rIGHt one!"

Both the Queen and King received some cheers from their armies, but people, for the most part, waited for the Outlander's response.

"But can't you hear—all of you—that it's the same name? It doesn't matter if you read and write from left to right or right to left—it's still exactly the same name!"

"Don't be *ridiculous.*" The Queen sneered across the hilltops. "*Of course* it's not. You *see*," she said, looking down to her troops, "she's just a *silly* little thing. She can't even tell the difference between two things being the *same* and two things being the *exact opposite.*"

Lee had just about had enough. Enough of the Queen and the King thinking they know better than everyone else. Enough of everyone not thinking for themselves and allowing the King and Queen to do their thinking for them. She was tired and sweaty and filthy and now, now she was just angry.

"Yeah, yeah, I've heard it all before. And you know what? That's just stupid! You can all just spell 'OVO' in capital letters, and there won't be anything left to fight over."

The armies went silent, digesting the novel concept.

"Wait!" yelled a woman from the crowed. "But what about the direction of spelling? The Eponymians write from left to right, and we write from right to left. Which one is correct?"

"It doesn't matter. That's the whole point." Lee tried to keep her patience.

"I have an idea," another woman yelled out. "We can both adopt a vertical alphabet and write from top to bottom."

"Why not bottom to top?" a man chimed in.

"I got it!" Another man, an older one, jiggled his finger up in the air for all to see. "We'll read and write in a circle. That way all spelling is equal."

"*Preposterous!*" the Queen snuffed, and, for once, Lee thought she was right.

"PreCIsely!" And the King, for once, agreed with her. "THere are no CIrcles in 'ovO'. It is not for Us to doubt HIs will—we are simply FOllowing HIs law."

Óseo walked up behind Lee. "Talk sense tu fools and they call *yu* foolish, eh, niña?"

"Yeah!" came another voice from the crowd. "It's not our fault, either. It's Ovo's bidding."

Percy joined Lee's side. They looked down at the buzzing sea of faces.

"People!" He waved up his hands, commanding the crowd with confidence. "The fault, dear friends, is not in your gods, but in yourselves. It is within *your* power to make peace."

"*HA!*" The King discharged a particularly dense cloud of smoke. "You WAnt us to make PEace? HOw can we make PEace with THem? THey're our Enemies."

The Eponymians and the Shibboletanians turned their heads as one, from the King to Percy and Lee.

"Well, that's how it works. You don't make peace with people who are already your friends. You make peace with your enemies, to turn them into friends." Lee scanned the crowd and was pleasantly surprised to see heads slowly beginning to nod, on both sides.

Mrs. Adocchiare joined Lee and Óseo and Percy at the peak of the hill. "I've always said, out of the mouth of babes wisdom springs forth." She smiled at Lee.

"REally. WEll, if THe girl is so sMArt," the King said, sneering, "WHose law do we follow THen, HUh? WHich rules do we go by?"

Mrs. Adocchiare smiled at him, almost amused. "All the rules you need to go by, dearies," she said, turning to the people below, "are those of goodwill, and hard work, and keen study. Everything else you can figure out later."

"So, this peace thing," a large soldier said, taking off his spiked helmet. Lee instantly recognized the man who had tried to kill her. "How does it work? Who stops fighting first?"

"You both do. At the same time," Lee answered him.

"Oh." He was still catching up to the idea. "So what do we do if the Queen, or the King, order us to fight?"

Lee looked at the two monarchs. They were livid at this very unwelcome turn of events.

"Well, do you like them?" she asked both armies.

A wave of debate rippled through the sea of people, gushing between the hills for a long moment.

"No. Not really," a woman answered.

The King and Queen's faces dropped. Lee thought the Queen might have said something, but even if she did, it was swallowed up by the commotion of approval.

"What do we do with them then?" someone asked.

"I don't know," Lee mumbled, "that's for you to decide. I guess th—"

"We should punish them!" someone else shouted, bringing about roars of agreement.

"Yeah! I say we throw them both off a high cliff!"

"How about stretching them on the rack?"

"No—we should tie them to tables, dip them in honey, and let goats lick them to the bone. Goats have tongues like sandpaper, you know!"

"But where do we get goats from? I have a better one—why don't we tie bottomless cages to their stomachs, and put rats in the cages, so the rats can tunnel through them to escape."

Lee tried protesting, as did the rest of her friends, but the crowd was too loud.

"I say dethrown them!" a soldier yelled out—the King's driver, no less, standing up in the car, right in front of the shocked King. "The Outlander is right. Both Eponymia and Shibbolet are a mess. I say we judge them to hard labor; that's a fitting sentence for waging this war for so long. Let them travel around both our kingdoms and clean up all the wreckage left behind in battles."

The crowed cheered as one. Lee looked to Percy on her left, and he winked at her, and to Óseo on her right, and he winked at her as well.

"Don't be *ridiculous*. That'll take an *eternity!*" the Queen objected with every ounce of her enormous mass.

"Yes, SHe's rIGHt. It's outLAndish!" the King went *puff—puff—puff.*

"That's okay." A member of Her Majesty's personal guard snickered. "There's no hurry."

And the sea below laughed—not a vindictive laugh, but a laugh of relief.

"So who will lead us now?" a young boy asked.

Grandmaster Phineas walked in front of Lee, clicked his heels, and extended his arm at her. "Ladies and gentlemen, brave souls of Elsewhere... I, Grandmaster Phineas, recommend that we resolve to make the ravishing Lee the rightful ruler of both our respective kingdoms. She has shown resplendent wisdom, righteous heart, and regal and refined manner. She is held by one and all in the highest regard. Is she not the most reasonable replacement?"

The crowd erupted in cheers again, this time louder and longer. They all stretched up in applause—not a single objection. Cries of support and adulation rung from both armies, like fireworks going off between the hills.

"Your Royal Highness." Grandmaster Phineas bent down on one knee in front of her. Everyone standing below did as well; a gathering of hundreds— men and women, young and old, Eponymians and Shibboletanians—all kneeled before her.

Grandmaster Phineas stood back up and turned to face the crowd. "*Long live Lee!*"

"*Long live Lee! Long live Lee! Long live Lee!*" The chant took over in a giant tidal wave.

Lee didn't know what to do. Never had she bargained on becoming a queen, and with two kingdoms to rule no less. She looked to her friends, pleading with her eyes for them to tell her what she should do. But they just smiled at her, offering no opinion but great pride.

She'd make a good queen, with time, she thought to herself. A fair and just queen. But, before her responsibilities as a queen, or even a princess, she had a much more important responsibility.

"Thank you. All of you," she said, trying to sound as royal as possible. "I'm very flattered. It's a great honor. But I'm sorry, I can't accept your offer. I haven't found my father yet. And, I don't think I'd make a good queen if I'm not a good daughter."

"What do we do? Who'll lead us then?" the giant man with the giant spikes called out.

The crowd joined in, calling for an answer. But she had none.

"Moi." Madame Couronne suddenly stepped up from behind her. There was no arrogance in her, no air of superiority.

"You?" Percy was astonished, his bushy eyebrows almost popping off his head.

"What can I say? Someone has to do it. And after all, I *was* a Duchess of ze royal court, seventh in succession to ze crown of France, n'est-ce pas?" She allowed herself to smile a full smile. She looked at Lee, who nodded eagerly. She looked dirty and tired, her velvet gown stained and torn in places, her head toppled almost completely over on its pillow inside a smudged and dusty jar. Yet she looked graceful and beautiful. She looked like a Queen.

Óseo offered her a slight bow. "Yur a woman of decency. Yur head may not be in the right place, but yur heart is. Je je je."

She responded with a small bow of her own. "C'est la vie. C'est la mort. C'est la même chose." She faced the crowd. "People of Elsewhere, I will be honored to be your Queen, if you will have me."

The people gave her their answer in a wave of applause and cheers. And there, on a hilly battlefield in Elsewhere, surrounded by a few old friends and many new ones, Madame Couronne finally had her coronation.

"Well, seems we've won the day at last, eh?" Percy's mustache wiggled.

"Just goes to show," Mrs. Adocchiare said, trying rather unsuccessfully to pat down Lee's ruffled hair, "never doubt the power of a few dedicated people to change the way of things. What else ever has, really?"

Lee agreed, and the four of them traded waves goodbye with the people of Eponymia and Shibbolet, and with Grandmaster Phineas and Sõt and even Sulyok, who hissed back, and with the newly appointed Queen Couronne, and started making their way down the hill to continue their search for Lee's father.

"Wait!" A familiar voice, like dewdrops, clear and shimmering, called from behind. "I'm coming wiz you."

"But you can't, dear. You're the Queen now," Mrs. Adocchiare said.

"Exactly. And as my first act as Queen, I appoint Grandmaster Phineas as my royal advisor." She turned to him. "Chevalier Phineas, I am entrusting you wiz ze government of my kingdoms until such time as my return."

"Oh. Of course, Your Majesty." He bowed deeply, a number of times, with unconcealed glee.

Queen Couronne joined them, and they walked off the hill, leaving Chevalier Phineas and his own newly appointed aid, Sõt, to the task of putting the affairs of the joint kingdoms in order. Lee glanced at Queen Couronne, trying to decipher her reasons for continuing the journey with them. The new Queen flashed another smile. "I made you a promise, mon petite chou, zat I will help you find your fazer. And I will not have it be said zat ze Queen is not a woman of her word, oui?"

Lee smiled. "Ok, then. We've wasted enough time here. Let's go!"

"Ha!" Percy let out a bark. "A precocious child, you are."

Lee smiled again. Of course she was. She was her father's daughter, after all.

XI

Two days and a night had passed by Lee's count. The miles blurred beneath their feet, across wide prairies, across land made entirely of jagged volcanic rock, across a dense canyon of colossal stalagmites, across terrain blanketed with odd flowers that colored everything in sight in blinding-bright orange. They walked keeping Eponymia and Shibbolet at their backs.

They passed the time telling stories about their lives and loved ones. Percy regaled Lee with tales of his adventures around the world, which the rest had heard countless times before. Mrs. Adocchiare came from a very large family in Italy, and had, last she knew, two brothers, four children, twelve grandchildren, nine nieces and nephews and twenty-two great-nieces and nephews, and they'd all lived in the same town. Queen Couronne talked longingly about life in the royal court before the Revolution, and Óseo preferred to share funny stories about his mischief as a boy in Spain.

Lee told them about the world and how it had changed since they died, which they found more astonishing than anything they'd seen since leaving their room in the darkness, but they were more eager to hear about her own life. She told them about her dad, who always had time for her, no matter how busy he was, and whose favorite food was ice cream, in almost any flavor. She told them about her mom, who loved visiting new places and seeing new things, sometimes just with her, and how she'd been working so hard since her dad died. She told them about Ron, who, despite liking to tease her a lot, was really a good big brother, but was never home anymore since they moved, and would never say where he's going or when he'd get back. She told them how her dad had died from a heart attack, suddenly and without warning, and how much they all missed him. But she was going to bring him back, and they would all be together again.

On the late morning of the third day, they came across a road and followed it until it split around a small stream of fresh water. Lee was parched by now and gulped as much of it as she could.

"Ye'll drink tha brook dry, lass."

She hopped to her feet. A very tall and gangly man stood a few yards away, smiling at her an enormous smile.

"Bonjour, Monsieur," Queen Couronne greeted him.

"Guid mornin folk. Hou's it gaun?" He made his way to them in three long-legged strides. "A'm Gordon. Bin ma friends call me Gingi, onaccount o me hair bein as red as ginger."

His smile, which seemed perpetual, was surrounded by a million freckles. His eyes were the green of the inside of a melon, and his hair was a big, unruly tuft of brilliant red. It looked almost too heavy for his gaunt neck to carry. A maroon and bottle green plaid kilt wrapped sloppily across his body, giving him the general appearance of an unmade bed. He walked with a long shepherd's stick, the kind that curved at the end.

"I say, good fellow," Percy said.

"Och! An Englishman, ar ye?" He reached out to him.

"Yes, indeed, sir." Percy smiled and shook his hand. "The name's Percy. You're a Scotsman, I take it?"

"Aye. That A am. D'ye spaek Scots?"

"Not particularly well, I'm afraid."

Gordon, or Gingi, looked to the others, but they all shook their heads. He turned to Lee. "And whit's yer name, wee lass?"

"Lee."

Whimsically, with a slight bow, he scooped her hand to his lips. "Pleasure." She blushed. She liked how he rolled his 'R's, like Óseo, but different.

He repeated the same for Mrs. Adocchiare and straightened up for a hearty handshake with Óseo.

"Nice tae meit ye, Aseo."

"Óseo."

"Hmm?"

"My name is Óseo, not Aseo."

"Sure." Gingi walked over to Queen Couronne, who, whether noticing the dirt on his hands or due to her new stature, preferred to bow instead.

A big, shaggy, woofing thing came running down the stream from behind some trees, wagging its tail so enthusiastically Lee was surprised it didn't take flight like a helicopter.

"Och! This burly thing haur is me dog, Bampot. Say awrite, Bampot."

"Whoof!" The dog barked, loud and friendly. Óseo recoiled a little, but Lee wasn't nervous at all. She reached to pet him, but he was far more interested in Óseo. He ran over and dug his snout under Óseo's pant leg, quickly pulling out one of his shin bones. Óseo tried to grab him, but he bounced away with the bone in his mouth, then turned around and bowed with his backside raised high in the air and his helicopter tail wagging furiously.

"Whoof!"

"A'm sairy, Aseo. Bampot juist wants te play wi's ye—"

"¡Óseo, not Aseo! And please tell yur perro loco tu give me back my leg." He balanced himself holding on to Mrs. Adocchiare's shoulder.

"Bampot! Gie's that!" Gingi pried the bone out of the dog's mouth, covered in drool. "Haur ye gae, gaud as new." He handed the dripping bone back to Óseo, who seemed like he just might let the dog keep it after all. He took the bone, wiped it off on his already stained white pants, bent down, and snapped it back into place with a small *click*.

Gingi smiled, apologetically but mostly amused, and turned to Lee and the others.

"Pneumonia."

"Beg your pardon?" said Percy.

"Pneumonia. That's whit did me in, whit A died from. Let me guess." He examined Queen Couronne, Percy, Mrs. Adocchiare, Lee, and Óseo, and, in that order, guessed, "Decapitation, drownin, snake bite, polio, an fire. Hou'd A do?"

"Not well, I'm afraid, my good man," said Percy. "You got the first one right, but I'd say that one's rather obvious, eh?"

"Aye."

Queen Couronne did not share their amusement.

"Gingi, do you know which road we should take?" Lee asked, pointing at the divergence.

"Whaur d'ye want te go?" he returned.

"I don't know," Lee answered.

"Then it disn't really matter, dis it?"

She liked Gingi. She could tell he was one of those rare adults whose behavior reflected their feelings and words reflected their thoughts. "I'm looking for my dad. Someone told me that people who died recently arrive on the other side of Elsewhere."

"O course!" He nodded. "As luck would have it, A ken exactly whaur the Other Side is. An whaur would the Other Side be, anywey, if not Elsewhaur?"

"Really?" She perked up. Things were finally starting to look promising.

"Aye! Been thaur many a time. Bin A dinna kin if ye're faither's thaur; tis a labyrinth, no ane can enter withoot bein invited."

"That's okay. I'll find a way in," she said with confidence.

"Ha! Ye're a sassy lassie, arn't ye? Well, tis thataway." He pointed his long arm down one of the roads. He thought it over for a minute. "Bin A tell ye whit, bairn. Come wi's, A'll take ye thaur."

"Oh, that's very kind of you sir," said Mrs. Adocchiare.

"We wouldn't want to impose upon you. You've been more than helpful already," said Percy.

"Yes," Queen Couronne agreed, "zere really is no need. I'm sure we will find it." Lee knew she wasn't just being polite, but preferred to make the rest of the way without the shepherd and his Shetland.

"Dinnae be glaikit. Tis nae problem."

"Yu sure?" Óseo asked, cautiously. He liked Gingi just fine, it was Bampot he could do without.

"Aye, thatsnaeborra—whit ar freends for?"

"I heartily agree. Capital of you, good sport." Percy patted him on the back. "How fortuitous that we happened to come upon our new friend here in our hour of need, eh?"

"C'est magnifique." Queen Couronne dripped sarcasm.

"Well," said Gingi, brightly, "dinna stand thaur like a tree—ye'll grow roots." He whistled for Bampot and started strolling down the road. "Coorie up!"

Lee walked next to Gingi, who walked at a leisurely pace, whistling a long, happy melody, which made the sky seem a brighter blue, the leaves a more vibrant green, and the rustling of the air among them perfectly in tune.

The path they followed was not much more than a strip of golden brown sand. When they crested the first high peak, Lee could see it winding until it was out of sight.

"Are we going to get to the Other Side today?" she asked.

"Aye, that we shall," Gingi answered and went back to whistling a new tune, a variation of pretty much the old one.

He walked in long strides, and Lee trotted beside him, inquiring every couple of miles whether they were close.

"Nae, wean. Inna spell," he repeated, never annoyed.

"You sure?" she eventually asked. It was nearing dusk.

"Sure as me kilt stays down cause o gravity!" He chortled. "An ye canna argue wi's gravity, now can ye?"

"Je le jure!" Queen Couronne tapped the side of her jar, producing a short *ting*. "For men, puberty does not end even after death. We have enough infantile humor from Óseo." Óseo looked at her and seemed pretty pleased with himself. "What are you grinning like a goblin for? It was not a compliment." She huffed at him, returning her attention to herself.

"Sae," Gingi turned to Lee. He had finished his latest whistle and seemed like he wanted a break. "Hou d'ye kin yer faither's in Elsewhaur? Hou'd ye git haur? An hou d'yeall meet?"

She shared her story with Gingi.

"Och! Yer alive?! A dinna believe it. Yer walkin aboot like iverything's normal. Verra streenge."

A live girl travelling in the company of the dead was a strange thing indeed, she agreed. Even more so from the perspective of the dead.

"Aye, tis a pretty kettle of fish, bonny lass. A howp ye succeed—A wish ye the best o luck."

"Thanks, Gingi. I will." she assured him and herself. "You know, whether you believe you can do a thing or not, you're right."

"Och-och! Wise in the weys o the world ye ar, ar ye nou? Ye kin," he said, turning to the four walking behind, "kids theday growe up fester thin whit thay uised te. Or is't the other wey aroond? A keep forgittin."

"Have you liv—been here long?" Lee asked.

"Aye! A'v been haur in Elsewhaur syne a lang time aby. A didna coont, bin A rackon a couple o centuries at least. Ye kin, A wis the maist famous shepherd in all o Scotland. Faur-kent, the name o Gordon Alba—that's me, wean—was respectit. E'en te this day A'm shuir men tell thair tall tales o me great deeds. Tis true as the light in the nuin, tis." He grinned.

They had been walking for hours now, following the road, which glistened golden in the fading light. Her stomach found this a good time to rumble in protest of its neglect, loud enough for all within earshot.

"Bonny lass, ye guttin?"

She nodded and reached into her bag for an apple, deliberated, and settled on yellow.

"A'll tell ye whit, wee lass—A got me some haggis left in me poke, if ye want. Made it meself. It'll fill ye better than aiples, that's for shuir."

"What's that?" she asked.

"Tis chopped lamm's heart, lungs, and liver, mixed for guid meisur wis shuet, aits, ingans, and pungent seasonings, then packed inte a round sausage skin made o cleaned sheep's entrails, and boiled te perfection. Tis verra guid for ye—it growes hair on the chest!"

"Um, no thank you. I'm okay. But thank you for offering," she said, hoping not to offend him.

"Hou aboot ye?" Gingi swung his head to Queen Couronne, who had been keeping to herself for the better part of the day.

"Certainly not," she said, indignantly.

"Suit yerselves, lassies. Yer missin oot."

"I expect I shall make do," she answered.

"Och, thatweewummansarightnippysweetie," he streamed out, chortling in good spirit.

"You're a fellow of good humour, Gingi," said Percy. "But nightfall fast approaches—how close are we to our destination?"

"Dinna fash yersel, tis juist a wee bit o a stride furthaur. We'll get thaur inna spell."

"Now listen, Gingi," Óseo said. He wasn't all too satisfied with the lackadaisical answer. "We've been walking all day. My bones are hurting." He kicked his foot up to point at it: little pebbles, lumps of dirt, and grass poked out from between the thin bones. "How far is it, du yu know?"

No sooner did he finish the sentence than a blur of a big, furry thing jumped across his path, leaving him holding up a footless leg.

"Och! Bampot, have ye no shame, ye messan dog? Gieve Aseo his foot back right nou."

Óseo reached out and grabbed Percy's hand, saving himself from an unpleasant fall. Bampot didn't seem to mind much his master's orders—with foot in mouth and tail wiggling, he ran up ahead of them to a bend in the road and started kicking up the dirt, digging a hole in the ground.

"¡Caramba! The dog is burying my foot," Óseo called, panicked.

Lee ran up to Bampot, and after a short tug-of-war, pried it out of his jaws.

"Whoof!" Bampot protested.

She handed it back to Óseo, who flopped it to the ground and pressed his stump leg into it.

"*Óseo*, yu loco shepherd," he said through gnashing teeth, "¡not Aseo!"

"A'm sairy. Tis been auld lang syne Bampot haur had a new freend te play with. But A daed as A promised; haur ye gae, tis over thaur—the Other Side."

They hurried up the bending road, looking to see where Gingi was pointing. Stretching across the entire horizon was a giant, continuous, silver wall. It loomed high above them, up into the sky, going on as far as the eye could see. It had no gates, or doors, or windows, or any other interruptions to its perfectly polished surface. It seemed impossible for them not to have noticed the wall before, and yet, not until they had cleared the curve in the road did they see it.

Gingi enjoyed their astonished reactions. "A'll be leavin ye folk nou. A better git back te me flock. Guid cheerio the nou!"

Lee didn't remember seeing any sheep. She gave a warm wave. "Goodbye. Thanks for everything."

The others waved as well. "Cheerio!" said Percy.

"Ye're welcome, freends. Lang may yer lum reek, sassy lassie!" He smiled broadly and, with Bampot at his side, went back down the road, his red hair disappearing behind the bushes as fast as the red head of a lit match.

"He's a jolly good fellow, that one. What?" Percy said.

"Pfft. Too tall for blood to reach his brain." Queen Couronne sneered.

Up close, the wall was absolute. It was utterly impenetrable, solid as fortified steel. Lee put her hand on it; it was neither hard nor soft, nor warm nor cold.

"Egad!" Percy gasped.

"What in ze devil's clawed hooves is zis?" Queen Couronne put her hand next to Lee's, stroking the wall.

"I confess I'm at a loss." Percy looked up and around. "Bewildering, indeed."

"¿Yu think yur father is maybe on the Other Side of this wall, niña?" Óseo said.

She stared at the wall for a long moment. "No. He wouldn't have come here. But that is where I'm going to find him."

"¿Qué?" He pushed the hat back on his head.

"It's where I'm going to finally find out where he is. They'd know."

"They? Who's 'they,' dear?" Mrs. Adocchiare asked.

"They. Whoever's on the Other Side." She looked at her friends. This may have been another obstacle

151

in her path, but it was also the first real clue to his whereabouts, she knew. She filled up with anticipation. "I need to get there. What should I do?" She hoped they'd have an idea.

Percy stroked his mustache, filing an edge. "A conundrum most vexing. There ought to be a secret passage somewhere to be found, a hidden door or the like, I'd wager."

"I razer doubt it," Queen Couronne disagreed. "Zis barrier is meant to be impassable."

"Perhaps we should look around? Maybe we'll get lucky and find something," Mrs. Adocchiare suggested.

Lee agreed. They started following the length of the wall, searching closely for clues. They walked in one direction for a while, then returned and walked the other way—but they found nothing. And what little light there was, was now gone.

Lee wondered who had built the wall and why. She wondered how deep it went into the ground. She looked down, and, to her surprise, discovered the wall ended a fraction of an inch above the ground. Light seeped under it.

"It's floating," she said, excited. "It's a floating wall. It's not touching the ground!"

"A levitating wall." Percy's brow stretched up. He leaned backwards, reexamining it, as if there was a clue he had missed at first glance.

Óseo bent down to look. "¡Locura!"

"Hmm. Madness indeed, old chum." Percy now stroked the other half of his mustache. "Yet there is method in it; only a mind unconventional in its perspicaciousness would come to find this sliver of an opening. It must be a test of sorts."

She tried digging her hand under the wall. The earth was hard, like grout, breaking up between her fingers into grains. Percy and Mrs. Adocchiare kneeled down to help her dig. Óseo tried, but his boney fingertips were no match for the tough soil. Queen Couronne looked at her hands, her milk-smooth skin and still mostly polished fingernails, and gave Lee an apologetic smile.

Lee burrowed her fingers deep, applying as much force as she could. They bruised and scraped, but little by little, the space beneath the wall widened.

She stood up and looked at the hole, just wide enough for her—not even Óseo—to pass through. She looked at the others uneasily.

"Have at it." Percy nodded in reassurance. "We shall await right here. But do mind yourself, will you?"

She took off her bag, leaving it with Óseo, and slid herself under the wall, head first. The opening was very narrow, and, to her surprise, it went on quite farther than she'd expected, definitely farther than she'd dug. She found herself crawling through a tunnel, under a wall as wide as a ship. The tunnel grew narrower and narrower, more suffocating. There was hardly enough air for her to breath. She looked toward where she had entered. There was nothing there, only blackness. Ahead of her there was only a stretch of light, still far away. She tilted her head sideways and started wriggling toward it. The tunnel slowly pressed the air out of her. It suddenly occurred to her that if the opening on the other end was not wider, she would be stuck. Unable to climb out, unable to turn back. But she had no choice. She neared the beam of light on the Other Side. Her lungs screamed for air. Finally, she reached the end of the tunnel. But her fears proved true—there was barely a sliver of an opening. Panic overtook her. She tried moving sideways, but it was too tight. On impulse, she grabbed the bottom edge of the wall and pulled with all her strength. She moved. She pulled harder. She moved some more. The soil was soft. In one desperate heave, she dragged herself out the Other Side of the wall.

She felt faint. She leaned against the wall, closing her eyes.

When she opened them, she had no idea how much time had passed. Maybe seconds, maybe minutes, maybe longer. She noticed for the first time her surroundings: a garden maze made of tall dark green shrubbery. The light all around was blinding, canvas-white. It cast deep shadows off the tall hedges, in which she could make out the details of the maze.

There were small pebbles sunk into the ground in cracked craters and big rocks suspended in the air at different heights. She touched one floating by. It skipped lightly, like a balloon. She kicked at a chestnut-size pebble on the ground. It didn't budge.

She walked with caution through the labyrinth, trying to memorize shapes and shades so she could find her way back. But time after time, as soon as she'd turn a corner, she'd find herself at the same spot she had just left, or the one before that, or the one before that. So she decided to try running and see where that took her. She marked an X in the dirt with her foot, chose a direction, and ran down it, then arrived at the X from another. She tried it again, faster, hoping that maybe speed would make a difference. This time she arrived just in time to see the back of herself running down the opposite path. She thought that maybe there was a trick mirror, but her other self took the corner just as she stopped.

Since running didn't get her anywhere, she tried walking slowly. That seemed to work better—she finally advanced down the intersecting corridors. Several times, when she'd reach an impasse and turn back around, she'd see herself again, as if she was catching a glimpse of where she would be a moment later. She called a thought to mind, and her other self obeyed; she turned around and smiled at her. It was the friendliest of smiles, of course, but it still sent a shiver down her spine.

Time passed in the maze, contorted and out of rhythm. She felt her body grow tired, then energized, as if from a catnap she never took. She became hungry, then full, then thirsty, then quenched, then hungry again, all in the span of a few minutes. It was like the inside of a dream, but where the dream made the rules instead of the dreamer.

A figure, in a long crimson hooded cloak, suddenly walked past her. Only the man was walking on the shrub wall, parallel to the ground, above her. He turned a corner. She tried to catch up to him, but by the time she reached the corner he was already gone.

"Hello? Is anyone there?" she called out. "Hellooo?"

"ɔoolleH ɔoolleH ɔoolleH ɔoolleH" A child's voice, which she recognized as her own, echoed back in reverse. The tiny hairs on the back of her neck stood up. Goosebumps prickled her skin.

"Come," a soft whisper resonated through the maze. It was close.

"Come."

She followed the voice down the dark green corridors until she reached an open court, shaped like a hexagon, each of its open corners leading down a passageway. She walked in. There was no one there. Just a large, empty white space.

"Welcome."

She jumped like a startled cat, turning around to the voice behind her. A person, dressed in gleaming silver, stared at her. She could recognize it was a woman by her general shape, but otherwise the woman was covered head to toe, her face hidden behind a silver mask. She wore a large triangular hat adorned with little bells, which moved, but made no sound, as she turned her head.

"H-Hello," Lee stammered.

The woman in silver looked at her, as if considering the best response.

"Hello."

"I'm Lee. Wh—"

"Come," the woman said in no tone in particular and walked past her. Lee turned around. The space was no longer empty, but full of people in robes and masks, all bright and shiny and colorful. Most had long, curved noses. Many had crowns or beards of feathers.

Some had intricately embroidered hats or cloaks. They watched her as she walked among them.

There was something peculiar about the masks. Their eyeholes were odd. She looked closer and discovered that they weren't holes at all; they were actual eyes, as colorful as the people's outfits. Their masks weren't really masks then. Those were their faces.

A man with a porcelain-white face decorated in golden swirls and black musical notes leaned down toward her. He seemed to smile, but she wasn't sure.

"Hello. I'm Lee. Who are you?"

"We..." he said, pausing, "are the Volto Festas. Welcome to our home."

"You live in a maze?" she asked.

"Can some not feel safe and call home where others feel lost and call a maze?"

She nodded, and looked around. "Is… is this real?" She didn't mean just then. She meant her whole journey.

"What is real?" asked the woman in silver.

The Volto Festas looked at her, expecting an answer.

"Um, I don't know…" She tried to think. "Me, maybe?"

They all laughed, together, like a beehive.

She felt a little embarrassed. "The world?" She hazarded a guess.

A face of black velvet covered by a red veil tilted at her. "If real is your world, what of other worlds? Does real not include them?"

"I… I don't know," she mumbled. "I guess."

They kept quiet, patient. She realized they were waiting for her to continue. She thought about it some more, formulating what she felt was a satisfying response.

"Reality is what's true."

Silence. Eventually, a man with a white and red checkered face asked, "If reality is true, is imagination then false?"

"Yes." She was fairly confident.

"Can reality not be less true than imagination?" offered the woman next to the checkered man. She had three faces of ember, each in a different direction, making it impossible to tell in which direction exactly she was facing.

"How?" Lee wondered.

"Is truth not specific? Is it not limited to the thing which is true, and may not hold true to another thing?"

She agreed.

"Is imagination limited in this way? Can it not stay true to all things? Can stories, legends, fairytales, even dreams, not be truer than true?"

She wasn't sure about this. "So it's not important if something's real or not?"

The woman stayed quiet for a moment, then gave her answer. "Is it important that a story is real, or is it important that the lesson it has to teach us is real?"

She considered the idea and found that it fit comfortably in her head.

The Volto Festas started walking, to nowhere in particular. She followed along.

"If reality is less real than imagination, sometimes, is it not less real than thought, always?" the woman continued.

"I don't get it." Lee curled her mouth.

"Can you think of a perfect circle?"

"Sure."

"Can you paint a perfect circle?"

"Sure!" She smiled. She was good at circles.

"Would it truly be perfect? Would it have no imperfections, no matter how small?"

She mulled it over. "No. You're right. Maybe not perfect."

The woman gave a slow nod down her middle face. "So can perfection exist in reality, or only in thought? Is thought not real first, and reality follows?" She sat down on a long stone bench that hadn't been there until just then. Lee took a seat next to her, while the other Volto Festas stood around. She looked at the three-faced woman.

"Ca—may I ask you a question?"

The woman blinked black eyelids. "Question everything. Dismiss nothing. Learn something."

"How come your faces are masks? I mean, wouldn't you prefer to just be yourselves?" She hoped she wasn't being rude. Somehow, she knew that these appearances had been adopted for her benefit, to better communicate with her. A man in a pristine white robe, whose golden eyebrows curled upward and continued past his face as small wings, leaned in behind the woman. "People are least themselves when they talk in their own person. Give them a mask, and they will tell you the truth. You have come here seeking answers, and so we made our faces into masks, so we can show you our true selves."

She understood, kind of. "So, did you also make this maze for me? Would it look different if I wasn't here?"

Another man, this one wearing a long red and yellow jacket with a hat of long red and yellow feathers, bobbed his head around in a circular motion, as if it was bouncing off his neck.

"Everything looks different if you are not there to see it."

The Volto Festas, she understood, were the masters of this world on the Other Side of the wall. "Is it hard? Creating a world?" she asked, wondering.

The red and yellow man paused before answering. "Creating worlds is forty percent play and ninety percent work."

"But that's a hundred and thirty!"

The man looked at her, blinking yellow lids over red eyes. "Is it? We were never very good at math."

The sound of splashing water reached her ears all of a sudden, and she turned her head. At the empty center of the hexagon now stood a small garden fountain, shaped like a flower with water streaming over the stone petals down to its pool base.

"Drink." Gestured the red and yellow man.

"Thank you." She put her mouth to the stream and drank long. She was still covered in dirt, and exhausted, but she felt much better now, and her head was much clearer. It occurred to her that they would know the answer to another question.

"Is this all just a dream?"

Two mauve-faced women in magenta dresses, with rings of bright yellow flowers around their necks, tilted their heads at her in opposite directions. "What is a dream if not imagination and thought?"

Lee nodded.

"The question we ask *you* is to which of us does the dream belong? Are you dreaming us, or are we dreaming you?"

She thought about it, but couldn't really tell. She shook her head.

"Is there a difference?" asked the one.

"I… guess. Yes." She didn't like belonging to anyone else's dream.

"What is it?" asked the other.

"Well, it's kind of like as if we were both characters in a story, and you wanted to know which of us is the main character, right?"

The Volto Festas stared at her, their expressions revealing nothing.

"Are you not?" a man finally asked. His eyes were completely vertical, midnight blue over gleaming silver.

"Not what?" She didn't follow.

"The main character. Are you not the main character in your story?" he asked again.

"I… I don't think so. I don't have a story, really. I'm just trying to find my dad."

The man paused, longer than the others. "Every person that ever was, is, and will be; every person that could, should, or might have been; every single one has a story. And each story is comprised of countless other stories, shorter ones; and most of those stories are shared by more than one person. So each of us is a character in someone else's story, just as others play a role in ours.

All these stories extend and connect to each other, and so each person's story relates to another's, and so all people tell their part in one big never-ending story."

Lee's mind stretched to contain the thought.

"Are you real people?" she asked without thinking.

They wobbled their heads collectively. "Not... in the way you are familiar with. More like..." A man in a black and gold cloak considered his answer. "Personalities. Ideas. Thoughts. Memories. Does that make us less real?"

"I guess not," she answered.

The man seemed to smile, but it was hard to tell with them. "Those are the only things that are truly real, by our definition. The rest is simply a vessel for them."

"You mean like a soul in a body?"

"If you will."

She contemplated the idea. Perhaps, then, all this was her soul leaving her body while she slept to travel the worlds of the afterlife. Perhaps her body was still curled up in the back of her closet. Either way, she knew this was no place for a live girl. She needed to find her dad, soon.

"Can you please tell me where I can find my father?" she asked.

"Have you searched Nowhere?" said the white-robed man.

"Yes."

"Have you searched Elsewhere?"

"Yes."

He waited.

"There are other places, aren't there?" she realized. "Then… where else?"

"Wherever."

She hesitated, unsure. "Is that another land?"

"Not exactly. You are thinking about it the wrong way."

"How?"

"Nowhere and Elsewhere are places. They are *some*wheres. Wherever is not a place; it is *any*where. It is more of a—" He seemed to be at a dead end. "It is difficult to explain. There is no word for it in your language. In any language, for that matter. But it is the *ever* part, not the *where*, that is important. That is where people go, in the end. That is where they spend the *ever*-after. Wherever."

She understood, even without fully understanding.

"Is it heaven? Do only good people go there?" Her dad was a very good man.

"We do not know," said a woman in green.

"How come?"

"It is the great unknown, even to us. We could just as easily have it all wrong."

She was not at all assured by this, but she was confident that was where her dad was waiting for her. And that was enough.

"But you do know how I can get there, right?"

The woman shook her head. "Our own wisdom is of no account—a shadow of a dream. We are wordsmiths. Thoughtsmiths. What you seek is the Machinesmith. The creator of things. He will help you get to Wherever."

Lee nodded, gravely. "Okay. Do you know how I can find him?"

They all remained silent for a long time. "Yes. He is not far. You are nearing the end of your journey. But be warned—it is a perilous journey. And at its end, there is a truth beneath reality."

The Volto Festas stood still, looking at her. The silver woman with the large belled hat who first greeted her stepped forward.

"Come."

Lee followed her out of the maze in a matter of minutes, arriving at the silver wall. It was still infinitely large and infinitely solid. She turned to the woman, about to ask if there was another way out besides crawling under it again, but the woman was gone. She turned back to the wall, and now it was gone. She found herself standing amidst her friends. It was still night. They were all asleep, leaning against the wall that was now behind her. Queen Couronne's snoring reverberating in her jar was the only sound around. Lee yawned and curled up next to Mrs. Adocchiare, who was always warm, placed her head in her lap, and fell asleep.

XII

Morning was cold and gray. A gust of frosty wind woke Lee up. The others were still sleeping and didn't seem to feel the cold. She sat up and shook Mrs. Adocchiare awake. She slowly opened her eyes, her left eye rolling outward toward the corner. Lee waved hello.

"Oh dear, dear! You're back." She smiled and leaned against Lee to haul herself up. The others stirred awake.

"Ah! You've returned to us. Very good. How went it?" said Percy.

"My brain feels like it's spinning inside my head," Lee grumbled. She gave them a detailed account of what she had found on the Other Side.

Percy listened attentively, nodding and playing with his mustache. "Indeed, we are such stuff as dreams are made on."

"They remind me of Las Fallas." Óseo rubbed his eye sockets and stretched his arms out.

"You know, dear," said Mrs. Adocchiare, "you were gone for three days."

Lee nodded, only a little surprised.

"Ha!" Percy was amused by her reaction. "A precocious child, of that there is no doubt. Very well—onwards we press then."

They set out in the direction the silver-faced woman had pointed out. The countryside was flat, and desolate, and cold. They marched for long hours across the plain, as the sky slowly turned from a harsh, colorless glow into the blood orange of another twilight. Percy regaled them with more stories of his wild adventures around the world, which Lee found vastly entertaining, though the others were clearly bored.

The temperature kept dropping as they pushed forward. It was cold enough that she could see her breath. Clumps of ice formed in the shadows of mounts and rocks, and soon snow began falling. Time passed. Snowflakes became flurries, flurries became fury. The wind whistled sharply, whipping her face.

"This is weather most foul!" Percy raised his voice over the wind. "We better reach shelter in short order."

They all agreed. Percy, Óseo, and Mrs. Adocchiare weren't as bothered by the cold as Lee, but Queen Couronne feared that her glass jar would freeze and crack. Lee's teeth were chattering so intensely that they hurt. The bitter cold wind reached through her pajamas, dug under her skin, grabbed her bones, and shook them painfully.

They trudged through the deep snow as the world turned completely white around them. The wind kept changing direction, whipping her from above, from the side, from the front. She tripped and fell into the snow, sinking ear deep. She jumped back to her feet and quickly brushed her face off. It was burning cold.

"Dash it! Are you all right? No, of course you're not," Percy shouted over the wind's wails. "We ought to gather kindling for the girl." But there was nothing but ice and snow all around.

"Poor dearheart." Mrs. Adocchiare rubbed her back.

Their route took them over a long, flat formation of ice bridging two cliffs a hundred feet above the ground. Despite the pushing, punishing wind, they made it to the other end. The ground was different there. The ice was thinner and smoother, and Lee could see dark water moving under their feet. They walked holding hands, shifting their weight carefully from foot to foot, step to step, cautious not to break the ice. Painfully slow, they eventually made it across the frozen water. Not long after the wind died down, and all was still again. The sky was indigo now, casting an eerie glow on the white surface below. She felt withered. It was hard to think straight. Her vision blurred around the edges.

"You look a bit frowzy, dear," Mrs. Adocchiare said.

"Pobrecita," Óseo said. He tucked his arm behind Lee for support and walked with her.

Several hours passed since they had left the arctic tundra. The air was much warmer now, the snow melted into puddles across the muddy earth. The sky was black. They could see a glow emanating in the distance, and they walked toward it. At last, they came upon a cluster of towers, rising against the night sky like a troop of giant mushrooms. The silhouette of a large city.

"My word!" Percy's jaw dropped as he took in the city's immense scale.

"Goodness gracious," said Mrs. Adocchiare.

"Ooh la la! Will you look at zat…" Queen Couronne exhaled a breath of awe. Lee realized they had never before seen such a big city. Neither had she.

"I hope they are friendly," said Óseo. "I du not care tu go through more fighting."

"You mustn't worry, old chum. Any man with a grain of wit will treat a decent suppliant like a brother."

"Maybe, Percival, but I prefer tu be careful. I think there is danger in this place. I can feel it in my bones." His smile was nervous.

They entered the city under a large neon green sign reading "ENTER," one of several spread out at equal distances across the boulevard. On their other side, facing inward, the signs read "EXIT" in neon red. All the streets and buildings in sight looked like they were built on a grid, everything constructed and set at straight angles. Lee could find no round shapes, no curves or arches or any soft lines of any kind. Queen Couronne noticed the exactness as well. "Efficiency, by its very nature, entertains very little quality, n'est pas?" Lee nodded.

The imposing buildings were colorless: cement-gray and stone-gray and steel-gray and glass-gray. There were no shops. No restaurants. And, Lee also noticed, no people in the streets. Through the windows of the buildings, however, swarms of figures moved about.

Some of the buildings, the taller ones toward the city's center, had sky bridges, like pipes, going between them. Long rails crossed the skyline, with trains stopping at designated towers. She could make out rows of people going in and out of the cars. Some of the trains even journeyed vertically, like elevators, along the sides of buildings, from street level to above the clouds and back.

All the structures in the city, from the smallest to the largest, without a single exception that she could spot, had giant clocks displayed prominently across their facades. No matter where they walked, there was always a clockface in line of sight: it was almost twelve of the clock, midnight, according to the city. But the streets were as bright as day, flooded with fierce white fluorescent pouring from continuous rows of streetlights. It hurt her eyes. Red and green neon signs everywhere displayed one-word directions like ENTER or EXIT or UP or DOWN or GO or STOP or OPEN or CLOSE or, in a few instances, simply YES or NO.

The air was miserably dank, "déplorable," according to Queen Couronne, and Lee's face was now covered in an uncomfortable mixture of grime and neon-induced sweat.

They arrived at what seemed to be the tallest building in the city, which went up until is disappeared into the clouds, its lights infusing them with a yellow glow. It also appeared to be the widest building, taking as much space as three or four of the others. Its entrance consisted of two gigantic metal draw gates. Above the gates hung a massive bronze plaque, its inscription set in thick, bold, cube-like letters:

GREAT IS THE WORLD AND ITS CREATOR. AND GREAT IS MAN.

A sudden noise startled them, like a short, sharp foghorn blow. An elevator train rushed down the side of the building across the street, coming to a stop with a loud *hsssshhhhhhhh*. Lee and the others took cover around a corner. The tower's gates rattled and opened slowly, revealing a hundred or more people, standing motionless, waiting. Green signs saying "IN" turned on over the sliding doors of four train cars, and the human mass marched, in order, military-style, out the large open gates and into the four open train cars. Lee noticed they all looked exactly the same; they wore identical charcoal-gray suits, the color of the buildings around them, one kind for the men, another for the women, and they wore their hair back, slick and tight against their scalps. When they had all boarded the train, its doors slid shut, the tower gates drew down, the neon signs went off, and the train shot back up.

"We should find someone tu talk tu," said Óseo. "Maybe there is a city hall here. See if they know where we can find this Machinesmith."

Lee and Percy nodded. "Mm-hmm. Concurred. But it seems the locals here are not given to walking about the streets. If it's answers we seek, I suggest we enter one of these gargantuan buildings," said Percy.

They looked around. None of them seemed to offer an accessible entrance.

"Hmmm," Percy mummed, displeased.

A sudden flare of white, like a camera flash, echoed between the city canyons. Then the sky roared, and a lukewarm shower washed the dirt off Lee's face.

"Oh, fiddlesticks!" Percy now was even more displeased. Lee didn't mind, though. For the first time in a long time, she felt clean. Óseo didn't seem too bothered either. "¡Está lloviendo a cántaros! ¡I'm getting soaked tu the bone, je je je je je!"

"We can go there." Mrs. Adocchiare pointed to a nearby building with a projecting ledge, and they ran under it.

Queen Couronne muttered irritably in French, holding up the flowery wide bottom of her dress, now weighed down by rainwater.

"Well, at least your jar is clean again," Lee offered.

Queen Couronne turned her head around on its lilac, golden-trimmed and peacock-feathered pillow, inspecting the jar around it. "Why yes, yes it is. Très bien."

Another piercing horn blow signaled the opening of the gates of two buildings, the one adjacent to theirs and the one across the street from it. Two long rows of people in gray switched buildings: each walked out the bowels of one under a red neon EXIT sign and into the bowels of the other under a green neon ENTER sign. Their motions were mechanical, coordinated, habitual.

Lee and Percy ran out into the downpour toward them.

"Hi there," said Lee.

"I beg your pardon, good madam," said Percy.

"Excuse me, sir—?" said Lee

"I say, good fellow! I say!" said Percy.

But they were completely ignored. No one slowed down. Stunned, they rejoined the others waiting under the ledge.

"Well," Queen Couronne said, grimacing, "so much for zat—"

"Halt!"

Three men in black uniforms rapidly strode up to them.

"You're under arrest. All of you."

"I'm sorry?" Mrs. Adocchiare wasn't sure she heard right.

"I said you're under arrest. Come with us. At once," one of the policemen growled.

Another lightning bolt pierced the sky above, followed closely by echoing thunderclaps that sounded like a thousand footsteps, frightening Lee even more.

"Zut alors!" Queen Couronne put her hand to her chest, gasping.

Percy kept his composure. "What are you babbling about? What on earth for? We have perpetrated no crime or offense, I assure you, sir. I demand to know the accusations."

The three policemen closed them in.

"The charges are illegal entry, vagrancy, loitering, attempted disturbance of work, harassment of working professionals, and dressing in unlawful colors."

"My good man, let me assure you this is all a simple misunderstanding. We are visitors to your fair town, simply passing through, you see. Please accept our sincerest apologies for any inconvenience we may have inadvertently caused, and with your permission, we shall now be on our way—"

"I said you are under arrest!" the policeman yelled, turning beet-red. "Take them away, men."

Percy's bushy white eyebrows soared up in astonishment, then swooped down in fury like a bird of prey. "Now listen here, you. I give you fair warning now—we shan't be treated this way."

"You can add resisting arrest to your list of charges, old man." One of the policemen sneered. They each grabbed an arm.

"How dare you. Unhand me at once, you ruffians, or I shall be forced to give you a sound thrashing!"

But the two just kept sneering, wrestling his arms behind his back. Lee wanted to jump in, but before she could decide what to do, Mrs. Adocchiare placed her hand on her shoulder, gesturing back at Percy.

"Manhandle me, will you? I'll give you a what-for. Have at you, rogues!" Despite being old, short, and portly, Percy moved with unexpected speed—swerving one leg behind one of the policeman's, and with a swift, powerful thrust, knocked him flat on his back. In an eyebat he then swung low, spinning around like a top, kicking up the other policeman's feet from under him, flipping him over. By the time the second policeman hit the hard pavement Percy was already on his feet, facing the third. He was close to twice Percy's size. He came at him swinging, but Percy evaded and blocked his blows with astonishing speed and agility, then slid between his long arms, and with one determined punch upwards, knocked him out, like a mallet ringing the bell at a "test your strength" carnival game. Lee could've sworn she even heard the *"piiinnnggg."*

"There," Percy said breathlessly, brushing off his hands. "We'll have no more of your tyranny." He turned around. Lee stared at him, dumbfounded.

"Ahem. Yes, well." He tugged on his shirt, straightening it, then tried to press down what little hair he had on the back of his head. "I mastered the discipline of acrobatic pugilism in my youth, whilst traveling the East Indies. Learned it from the dethroned Rajah of Mukkapoor himself, I did."

Lee remained speechless.

"Well, I couldn't very well abide by the Marquess of Queensberry's rules when faced with three assailants, now could I?"

She looked down at the three policemen. Two were unconscious, one was moaning.

"Quickly now, girl—while the getting's good, let's leave this den of iniquity. I do not wish to engage the entirety of the local constabulary."

"¡Arrea!" Óseo called out, already ahead, and the five of them escaped into the nearest street.

Cautiously, they navigated through the streets, trying to stay close to the walls of buildings. But there were no shadows to hide in, and the rain stopped as abruptly as it had begun. She still hadn't seen anyone walking up or down a street. She couldn't even find a building that looked like a residence; they were all offices.

They walked silently through a silent boulevard and found themselves back in the center of the city, in front of the giant building. Somehow, they'd made a full circle. Or square.

"Are you in town for business?" someone asked. They turned around quickly. The man was not a police officer but clearly a businessman, dressed in a sharp black suit with a matching tie over a bleached white shirt. He neither smiled nor frowned. His jet-black hair was coiffed back firmly, and he was immaculately clean-shaven. He looked almost alive, if not for his pale complexion and his eyes, sunken deep in his head and glazed with a sickly yellowish tint. He stood there alone.

"Bonjour." Queen Couronne decided to be the one to interact with the locals this time around. "Monsieur…?" She waited for a name.

"Mr. Toossik," he introduced himself, flatly.

"Enchanté." She nodded, offering a congenial smile. He nodded back. His eyes caught Lee's. They were unsettling.

"Painting is illegal here. You're carrying contraband." He gestured to the canvasses sticking out of her bag. His voice was very exact.

"I'm sorry," she said.

"We do apologize, Monsieur Toossik," Queen Couronne said. "We are not familiar wiz ze laws of your city. What is ze name of it?

"The City."

"Yes," she answered, assuming it was a question. He didn't bother to correct her. He just waited instead. "Ah, I see. It is called Ze City, oui?"

"None of you are up to code, you know."

"What code?" she asked.

"The dress code, of course. Black or gray over white shirts, business attire only. Are you in town for business?" he asked again.

"I am afraid not. I am a visiting dignitary, and zis is my entourage." She pointed briefly at Lee, Óseo, Percy, and Mrs. Adocchiare, keeping a formal air. "I am ze new Queen of Eponymia and Shibbolet, now united under my rule. Ze five of us are on our way somewhere else."

"It's an honor to have you with us, Your Majesty," Mr. Toossik said, bowing only as much as he felt he needed to.

"Now, I realize zat a... skirmish may have taken place between one of my servants and your local policier, but I should zink it would be a much better zing to put such silly nonsense in ze past, oui?"

"Of course, Your Majesty," Mr. Toossik agreed. "If I may, then, arrange for an escort for you and your party to your destination?"

"You may," Queen Couronne said.

"Follow me." He walked toward the giant building. "I'm afraid I'll have to hold on to that until you exit the city." He reached out for Lee's bag.

Queen Couronne and Percy both gave her a slight nod. Reluctantly, she surrendered it. He folded the strap, carrying it like a briefcase.

"So what else aren't you allowed to do here?" she questioned, unsure whether it was a proper thing to ask.

It wasn't. Mr. Toossik glared at her. "The law here is simple and strictly enforced. It is illegal to smile—"

"Huh? How come?" she interrupted.

"Because it contorts the human face to that of a monkey. Monkeys are also illegal, it goes without saying. So are bananas, climbing, swinging, or any such apish activity."

She wondered if this was Hell.

"It is also forbidden to grin, sing, yell, whistle, hum, purr, chirp, buzz, hoot, howl, holler, trill, shrill, snort, sneer, finger-tap, feet-patter, lip-smack, grunt in rhythm, tap or drum, stick your tongue out, or create any other disturbance of the kind that might interfere with the workday or night. Is that all clear?" he asked, dispassionately.

Lee had half a mind to answer. She was burning up with the urge to argue and point out the sheer ridiculousness of these laws. But sometimes saying nothing is the smartest thing to say.

"How absolutely horrid!" Mrs. Adocchiare tried to whisper in her ear, but Mr. Toossik heard her. His thick, jet-black eyebrows narrowed over his sickly yellow eyes.

"We work as a collective here in The City. Our laws must be strict. If everyone did whatever they wanted, no work would ever get done."

"So everyone in The City is a worker?" Lee asked.

"Of course not. There are no workers here. Everyone works, obviously. But The City employs only the brightest and finest professionals. If you work here, you are either an Administrator, a Manager, or, if you're truly industrious, an Executive."

"Then who does all the work?" she wondered.

"I told you." He was starting to show impatience. "The Administrators, Managers, and Executives."

"Then whose work do they supervise?" Lee wondered still.

"Their own. Why would they need to interfere with each other's work? That would be counterproductive, time-consuming, cost-prohibitive, and worst— unprofitable. I can see you people know very little about business."

"Do you take me for a yokel, sir?" Percy objected. "I was managing my family's vast finances when your grandfather was still soiling his nappies."

Mr. Toossik almost smiled. "Perhaps. But the resources of your family, as vast as they may have been, are insignificant compared to those of The City's Board of Directors, of which I am the Chairman. So you'll forgive me, servant to the Queen, if I remain unimpressed."

Percy leaned down to Lee, so close that his mustache tickled her ear. "This fellow has a lean and hungry look. Such men are dangerous," he whispered.

She peered at Mr. Toossik, at his perfectly polished shoes and perfectly slicked-back hair and perfectly pressed suit. She then noticed his back was crooked, resembling a question mark from the side.

"Mr. Toossik? I haven't seen any kids since we got here. Where are all the kids?" she asked.

"We don't have any." Mr. Toossik said in his exact voice.

"No children?" Óseo was surprised. "How can a city this big have no children?"

"We have no use for them." Mr. Toossik said. "They make poor Administrators, terrible Managers, and the worst Executives imaginable. They completely lack work ethic. I don't care much for them myself. Messy little things. A necessary evil, I suppose, if The City is to have its growing workforce. I'd just prefer if their gestation period into proper working adults was shorter.

Lee wasn't really surprised by this, though she was a little surprised that she wasn't. "Maybe…" She ventured to remark something clever, but they had reached the elevator train's stop as it came down, and Mr. Toossik signaled them to follow him in. The car was a vertical gray rectangle with no seats, just bars to hold on to. She looked out the window as they zoomed their way up the side of the building. She could see only a blurry grid of bright windows, until suddenly the view of the entire city spread out before her, only to be replaced a moment later by eerily lit clouds.

They got off at the last stop, at the top of the tower. It led directly into a very large room, with a long rectangle slab for a table and floor-to-ceiling windows. This was the Boardroom, Mr. Toossik explained. They were well above the clouds now.

Mr. Toossik turned to Queen Couronne. "Forgive me, Your Majesty, but I must ask that you surrender your servant girl to our custody. Your cooperation in the matter would be greatly appreciated."

"Excusez moi?!" She wrenched her head back in the jar. "I'm afraid I do not take your meaning, sir. What is ze meaning of zis?"

He looked at Lee. "I've neglected to mention another law of The City; children are illegal here. They are not only unproductive but downright disruptive. Particularly those with artistic tendencies, and especially those with the means to carry them out." He held up the bag of art supplies. "They simply can't be trusted, and I can't allow the chance of our personnel being exposed to this girl. I speak for the Board when I say that we're truly sorry. We are fully prepared to make whatever restitution is required, naturally."

"Now look here, you lout," Percy said, losing his temper. "We shall do no such thing. The girl shall remain in our care. And we demand safe passage out of this wretched municipality of yours, forthwith!"

Mr. Toossik stood unfazed. He then smacked a call bell resting on the large table, and a group of policemen, ten or twelve, entered the room. Lee recognized three of them; they were the officers Percy had fought earlier. The angry one was now fuming, dark veins stretching up his neck and temples like his face was pushing from out of a cobweb.

"Oh, my!" Mrs. Adocchiare said.

"¡Maldita sea!" Óseo said.

"No harm will befall her, I assure you," Mr. Toossik stated. "Like all other children in The City, she will be put through rigorous career training, right here in the Central Tower, until she is a consummate professional and ready to join the workforce."

"You lied!" Lee yelled out. "You do have kids here—they're just all locked up inside this building."

He looked at her, a sliver of a smile flashing through his ghostly yellow eyes. "Lying isn't against the law in The City. But yelling is."

"We find ourselves in dire straits yet again, it seems," Percy said.

The police—Lee counted an even dozen now—moved in to take her away. Queen Couronne shifted in front of her, puffing herself out to full size, and was about to say something, invoke her royal standing, probably, when the window closest to them shattered into a million little pieces, sending splinters and glass dust flying at the policemen and ringing Lee's ears.

Percy was the first to regain his senses. "Quickly! 'fore they see us in leg-irons!" He rushed them out the opening and onto the train platform. Mr. Toossik and his policemen slowly staggered to their feet. Shards of glass covered their black uniforms and imbedded their pale faces like pins in pincushions.

Already out on the platform, Lee stopped. Her bag was on the boardroom floor, halfway between her and Toossik. As terrifying as he was, she needed it to reach her father and to get back home. She ran back inside, the others calling after her, reached the bag and dashed back out. To her surprise, Mr. Toossik and his henchmen made no effort to catch her.

"You have nowhere to go," he said, monotone. He was right; the platform was nothing more than an open balcony, high above the ground. Her thought was interrupted by a large harpoon sailing inches from her head, lodging itself deep into the concrete wall above the shattered window. Attached to the harpoon was an extremely long metal cable disappearing down through the clouds. Five metal rings slid off the harpoon toward them. She understood immediately. "It's a zip line! C'mon." There was no time to think. She ran toward it, the others following, and in one fell swoop jumped to grab a ring and started sliding down the cable.

"¡Vamos!" Óseo rushed Mrs. Adocchiare and Queen Couronne to grab the next two, then grabbed one himself. Percy took the last one, yelling, "Tally-hoooooooooooooo!"

The ring was thick and hard to hold on to. Lee slid, first slowly, off the train platform, her feet dangling above the clouds, then zoomed down to pierce them. Cold drops pelted her face as she gathered momentum,

emerging from the clouds to her own screams. The Central Tower was like a giant, sheer cliff behind her. She was high above the city, terrifyingly high—everything below was so tiny that she couldn't make anything out, just a network of lights. As the city hurried to greet her, her mind tried to slow everything down. She passed the tallest rooftops, zipping down a narrow canyon of buildings at breakneck speed. She caught glimpses into the offices, filled with rows of people behind desks working in synchrony. She wondered where she'd stop. The incline of the cable moderated, its visible path ending in a dark alley ahead, the only darkened spot around. She could see now the streetlights and neon signs and hear the screams of her four friends right behind her. She zipped into the blacked-out alley and slammed onto the ground with a jolting force that knocked the air out of her. She hurt, all over, but she was still alive. Even her bag was in one piece. She had landed on a large pile of mattresses, several feet high. She got off quickly. The others landed right after her, thankfully without the sound of bones breaking or glass shattering. All of them had made it unharmed.

She tried looking around, but the alley was too dark. She could sense, though, that they were being watched.

"We should get out of here quickly, niña," Óseo said, and they headed toward the intersecting avenue. A group of people suddenly jumped out of the shadows. The brilliant lights of the avenue behind them blinded her; all she could make out were silhouettes. She grabbed Percy's hand; she could feel he was also tense.

But then, unexpectedly, the dark strangers scurried into one of the buildings, waving their hands for them to follow.

They were led quickly down one florescent-lit passageway, then another, then another. They couldn't still be in the building, she concluded. They were being ushered underground, beneath the streets.

A few hurried moments later, they arrived at a large windowless basement. A man was waiting for them there. He wore a frayed and faded shirt over shabby pants. His eyes were cloudy, but he studied them like a hawk.

"How're ya folks doin'? I hope yer landing wasn't too rough." His smile curled up the side of his face.

"Not at all, sir." Percy smiled back and shook his hand. "We are in your debt."

"It was a tricky rescue, I'll give ya that." The man nodded. "I'm Joseph, Joseph Gills. But ya folks can call me Joe."

"Very well, Joe. I'm Percy. This here is Lee, and Óseo, Mrs. Adocchiare, and Queen Couronne."

"Pleasure ta meet y'all. Now, ya must be wonderin' who I am and what this is all about, so let me fill ya in. I'm the leader of the resistance movement, and this here's our lair."

Lee and the others looked around. It didn't look like much.

"Well, ta be honest, it's more like a ragtag group of rebels, so far, but we're growin'—more folks are joinin' us every year. Here, let me introduce ya to the others." Joe called over a group of people, the same group from the alley. "This here's Flint; he's what ya call our firearms expert. He's the one who shot the harpoon up inta the tower."

"A splendid display of marksmanship, sir." Percy was impressed.

Flint gave a humble nod. He seemed perfectly nice, but his appearance startled Lee. He was shirtless, and his skin looked like a scorched tree trunk. Small fissures ran through the black crust, mostly around his neck and under his shoulders, pulsating orange-red with heat. When he moved, they sputtered specs of ember into the air around him, like fireflies.

The rest of the rebels were no less peculiar. Mbili was a tall, broad-shouldered, wide-featured man with long, thick dreadlocks, who spoke in a very deep voice and a deep accent, which Lee recognized to be African. He seemed to be cut in half; his torso kept sliding off his legs, which was why, she imagined, he had tied ropes around himself—between his legs and over his shoulders, then wrapped around that—so he wouldn't become separated.

Another rebel, a small woman named Ilea, wore a dark stained apron over her clothes. It sagged a little as she leaned, and Lee glimpsed behind it the woman's intestines, held in place by the apron.

The fifth revolutionary, a woman named Gara, stood quietly by the corner of the large basement. An air of melancholy surrounded her. Her arm was made up of sewn segments that had been forced together; her hand was attached at the wrong angle to her arm, and her shoulder was replaced by a bony, angular knee. Her entire body was a construction of mismatched puzzle pieces.

They all looked ghastly, but, Lee decided, seemed like good people. And besides, she was becoming accustomed to the dead.

"¿There's only five of yu? ¿That's it?" Óseo wondered. "Yu cannot mount a revolution with five rebeldes. That's like trying to build a boat with five planks of wood."

"Sure is," Joe admitted. "But if the five of us can figure out there's more ta death than work, maybe others can realize that, too. That's what we hope ta do—inspire the people."

"Why do you even bozer wiz ze ozer louts in zis city? You have your independence—why not just leave here?" Queen Couronne puzzled.

"We can't. What good is our own liberty if we ignore the oppression of others?" Joe answered. "Nope. We gotta do what we gotta do." The other rebels all nodded.

"Humph. A wise man cares pationately for ze opinion of a few, and has little use for ze opinion of ze rest." Queen Couronne curled her lip, hiding the littlest scribble of a smile.

"So why have you brought us here, Joe, if you don't mind the asking?" said Percy. "Clearly, there is much work yet to be done. But we really must be on our way—"

"Well, y'see, Mbili here was on a scoutin' mission when he saw ya folks bein' brought up ta the Central Tower, with the kid. We figured ya could use some rescuin', and, well, ta be honest, I was kinda hopin' a bunch of escapees such as yerselves might wanna join us."

"I'm afraid we cannot." Percy shook his head. "I am sorry, but this is not our fight. We've had enough warfare to last us an afterlifetime already."

Joe nodded, trying not to look too disappointed.

"Now, if you would be so kind as to direct us to the nearest exit to The City, we'd—"

"Percy, no! We have to help them. We have to," Lee interrupted. She thought of the people, going from one workplace to the next, then on to the next after that, never stopping, ever, forever. "We can't just leave here like that."

"Now, don't you get snippy with me, young lady," Percy snapped back. "In case you've forgotten, it is your father that we are searching for."

"Esta niña es de abrigo." Óseo rolled his eyes. "Listen, niña, the viejo is right; yu cannot help everyone. It is time tu move on."

"I know," she said. She wanted to help, but she desperately wanted to find her dad. She missed him so much. And now, finally, she was close. She just needed to find the Machinesmith, as the Volto Festas said. "I'm sorry. I just wish there was something we could do."

"There is."

She looked over at Mrs. Adocchiare, who flashed a smile. "Not every fight is won by fighting. I'd dare say the truly important ones rarely are."

"What do ya mean, lady?" asked Joe.

She waddled over to the side of the basement, where shelves full of supplies stood, and dragged back across the cement floor a long roll of fabric. All nine of them—Lee, Percy, Óseo, Queen Couronne, Joe, Flint, Mbili, Ilea, and Gara—watched her with increasing curiosity as she spread the cloth across the floor in front of her. She stood up and smiled at Lee, her eyes twinkling. "I told you angels sent you to us, dear."

Lee smiled back, though she was still baffled.

"There they are—the angels' footprints." Mrs. Adocchiare giggled, delighted once more by Lee's dimples. "Now, it's time for you to spread your wings, sweetheart."

Lee looked at her, trying to decipher her grin, then at the large fabric roll on the ground. It was three times as wide as she was tall, fairly smooth in texture, and very pale gray in color, almost white. She looked up to Mrs. Adocchiare again, and all of a sudden it dawned on her. She understood what Mrs. Adocchiare had in mind. She put down her bag and took out her paints and her widest brush. She bent down and started to paint.

She painted this way, hunched over braced on one hand, creating first a big circle, then another, then a third, in a triangular formation, each partly overlapping the others.

She filled in the first circle with her bright yellow. The second with blue. The third, red; where the yellow and blue circles overlaid, they created green; where the yellow and red circles overlaid, they created orange; where the red and the blue overlaid, they made purple; and in the middle, where all three circles overlapped, it was black—at the center of it all was darkness, containing all colors within it.

When Lee was done, she showed the painting to Joe and his band of rebels. She waited for them to say something, but they didn't say anything. They just stared at it astonished, struck with awe, as if they were witnessing a miracle. She understood. She had introduced something new to their world; primary colors, in round shapes. It was a symbol of something different and strange and rebellious. A symbol for the resistance.

"What… what is it?" Flint finally said.

Mrs. Adocchiare looked at it, prouder than if she had painted it herself. "Why, it's your flag, dear."

"How did you make that?" Joe asked Lee. She shrugged. It just seemed like the right thing to paint.

Mrs. Adocchiare gently patted her head. "Children find everything in nothing, adults find nothing in everything."

Lee knew she had managed to find a way to help after all. But her contentment was short-lived: she saw now that her paint tubes were almost completely empty. She had barely enough left for two paintings. One to find her father, one to get them home. There would be no room for mistakes.

Joe stared at the painting some more, then cut it from the roll, holding it up to the weak light. "A flag. Yes. And flags oughta be flown, right?"

"I du not like where this is going…" Óseo said.

Joe and the other rebels exchanged mischievous looks. "It's almost time for the shift change—if we hurry, we can hang this up right in front of the Central Tower, just in time for mornin' rush hour."

"Ha! You're an audacious lot, I'll grant you that." Percy chuckled, holding on to his round belly. He was about to add something, something that began with a "but," when his eyes met Lee's. "Oh, fiddlesticks." he moaned, shaking his head. "In for a penny, in for a pound, eh?" His walrus mustache curled up.

"I agree wiz ze squelette." Queen Couronne's head tipped further to the side, toward Óseo. "Zis is not our business."

"Exactly!" Mrs. Adocchiare started waddling her way out the basement door. "Not business at all." Everybody soon followed, and eventually so did Queen Couronne, mumbling in French.

Outside, it was raining again. The ten of them snuck between the clustered buildings, moving close against the walls like fleeting shadows. The rain came down not in little, individual drops, but in a multitude of thin, long cords that absorbed the dawning light and cast everything in gloomy dimness. Lee didn't think it was possible, but The City looked even grayer.

Joe and his rebels led them with confidence. They slipped in and out of streets and alleys until they finally stood in front of the giant gates of the Tower.

Lee handed Joe the rolled-up flag, which she had done her best to keep dry despite its size. As he took it, someone cleared their throat behind them, loud and slow. Mr. Toossik stood expressionless, shards of glass still sticking out his face, accompanied by his policemen.

"Mr. Toossik," Joe hissed through a clenched jaw.

"Mr. Gills."

Loud thunder rumbled through the empty street.

Another group of black-clad policemen came toward them, waving batons. They turned to run, but more barricaded their escape.

"I rather think this is where we make our stand, eh?" Percy coiled.

Lee looked around. There must have been a hundred of them.

"Psst!" Joe whispered out the side of his mouth, grabbing her and Percy's attention. "Keep him busy, willya? Keep talkin'."

"I shall endeavour to do so," Percy whispered back. He matched his gaze with Mr. Toossik's. "Óseo," he said, softly enough to be heard only by him and the others, "do you remember what a 'blatherskite' is?"

"¡Sí!" Óseo replied merrily.

"Well, let's have at it, shall we?"

Mr. Toossik observed them, calm as a sculpture.

"Hey, Señor Toossik," Óseo called out to him over the rain claps. "¿What du yu want from us? We have done yu no wrong."

"You've broken the law. But I'm not an unreasonable man. I'm willing to offer the four of you an official pardon. I just want the girl," he answered.

"Egads, man!" Percy snarled. "Why do you dunderheads obsess over her so? Why not simply let us be?"

"Yeah, why?" Lee demanded to know.

"Because you're different."

"What do you care if ze girl is different?" Queen Couronne asked. "Does everyone in Ze City have to be ze same?"

"Yes," he answered with conviction. "They do."

"Why?" Lee challenged. "We all look different." She didn't remember seeing any other walking skeletons or women carrying their head in a jar.

"You're a different kind of different. You're dangerous."

"But why?" she insisted.

He looked at her for a moment, through the rain. "Because all it takes is one. One exception to the rule. One anomaly to bring down the whole system. Like one wrong number in an equation."

"And all of this for work. Just so you can have better business." Mrs. Adocchiare joined in.

"No, you have it all wrong. Work is not a means, it is an end. One does not work so one may prosper in business. One prospers in business so one may work."

"Why, that's sheer lunacy, man," Percy cried out.

"¡Sí!" Óseo said. "I think yu are a few bubbles short of a soda."

"It's just business," Mr. Toossik answered. "Nothing personal."

"Well, if you ask me, instead of pursuing the business of business, you should be practicing the art of kindness," Mrs. Adocchiare huffed.

"You're funny," he responded without the slightest smile. All of a sudden, he looked up—something had grabbed his attention. Above the entrance to the Central Tower, covering the large bronze plaque, vividly illuminated by the glaring streetlights, was Lee's painting. He looked at it astonished, and then horrified, once he realized he couldn't do anything about it before the shifts changed. As if on cue, the piercing horn blow sounded, and a train came down the side of the building across the street.

In a matter of seconds, a red neon light saying "OUT" turned on above them as the giant gate drew open, and a green sign saying "IN" lit above the empty train cars. Even though the mass of people walked in files, and even though their backs were to the flag, and even though they kept their eyes straight ahead, and even though it was raining, someone had caught a glimpse of the flag. Maybe from the corner of their eye. Maybe in a reflection in one of the train windows. At first only a handful turned their heads, slowly. They stopped and stared. Others followed their gazes up to the flag, and they, too, stopped in place. Then more and more, then all, stood in the rain, mesmerized by the three primary-colored intersecting circles.

A second train came down across the street as the second gate of the Tower drew open. The green "IN" sign turned on above it, and the day shift walked out of the train. They noticed the flag hanging high in front of them. Nobody moved, in either direction. Nobody uttered a word. Lee could see it in their eyes—faint recognition. Like when encountering something strange, yet instinctively comforting.

"What are all of you standing there for, you have work to do!" Mr. Toossik barked, losing his composure. "Go about your business. *Go on!*"

But the crowd ignored him.

"You know, dearheart," Mrs. Adocchiare said to Lee, almost casually, "this is not a bad turnout for your first art exhibit, hmm?"

She giggled.

"You horrible, unmanageable little savage!" Mr. Toossik's yellow eyes glared. She could see their little blood vessels widening, turning them orange.

"Mr. Toossik," Joe called out to him. "You're fired!"

She burst out in laughter—a silly, goofy, untamed laugh that went from head to toe, until her sides hurt and she was out of breath and she could laugh no more. An illegal laugh. A contagious laugh. Like wildfire, it ignited every single person in a suit with pure and joyous and liberating laughter, in the middle of the street, in the rain, in front of the Central Tower of The City.

She didn't stay to see what happened next. They hurried away, leaving Mr. Toossik and his helpless police behind. Joe led them quickly through the streets, into a building, and down into the tunnels beneath.

"Casabel," Óseo said, grinning at her as they walked down a passageway, "yu still continue tu amaze me. Yu have given these people a wonderful gift, yu know."

She nodded, humbly, dripping wet.

"Hear, hear," Percy agreed. "You've given them a symbol to believe in. That is a most potent thing."

"Zat will do, I suppose." Queen Couronne nodded her head on its pillow, pouting. "It is now up to ze citizenry of Ze City."

"Oh, I have a feelin' things are gonna start changin' 'round here." Joe looked cheerful.

"Yes." Gara, who somehow had managed to keep pace despite her jagged limbs, made something of a nod.

Mrs. Adocchiare and Lee exchanged very pleased smiles.

Shortly, they came out of the tunnels into the daylight. It had stopped raining, and the streets were wet and empty. A large, red neon "EXIT" sign hung above them. They were at The City's border.

"Well, this is goodbye, then." Percy reached out and shook Joe's hand. He bent down to kiss Ilea and Gara's hand, then returned to handshakes with Mbili. With Flint he settled for a friendly salute.

"Ya sure we can't convince y'all ta stay? It's just about ta start getting' interestin'!" Joe chuckled.

Surprising everyone, Mrs. Adocchiare stepped forward. "I'll gladly do whatever I can to help, Joe."

"But… I thought we're all going to go find my dad together…" Lee failed to hide the disappointment in her voice. "I mean, I understand…." She paused. She knew this was the perfect place for Mrs. Adocchiare.

"Now, now, it's nothing to fuss about, dear." Mrs. Adocchiare's short, chubby fingers brushed through her hair. "I'm not staying here right now. I'll come back."

Lee beamed.

"Spreading the Good Gospel to the poor sods, I suppose?" Percy jeered.

Mrs. Adocchiare looked at him, smiled her grandmotherly smile, and—to his shock—pinched his plump cheek. "No, there's a time and a place for everything, Percy, and this isn't it. The people of this city have spent enough of their afterlives deprived of independent thought. I think less uniformity and more individuality are in order, wouldn't you agree?"

"Hum, yes, yes, of course," Percy mumbled, blushing.

Goodbyes and grateful pleasantries were exchanged, and Mrs. Adocchiare promised to come back and help with their cause as soon as Lee found her father and was safely on her way back home.

It was time to go find the Machinesmith.

XIII

Lee galloped and skipped, bouncing from Percy to Óseo to Mrs. Adocchiare to Queen Couronne. She couldn't help it. She was hopelessly restless. She was restlessly hopeful. Her journey to the unknown was coming to an end, and at that end her father awaited. She could sense it.

The sky was clear now, a blank canopy the color of honey. The ground was rocky and overgrown, with tall dark trees poking out from large piles of ashy leaves.

The five of them spent the day walking and talking, rehashing the events of the past few days.

Late in the afternoon, by her estimate, they came across a small, scruffy white and brown dog, about the size of a pillow, small enough for Óseo to not be too afraid. Its midsection was flattened, a black tire mark running across it. It sat down, its tongue drooping out, and stared at them.

"Hi there." Lee reached down her hand for it to sniff. She felt sorry for it, but she was glad dogs had a life after death, too.

Its mouth opened, and it yelped with its whole body, but no sound escaped. It then rose, scampered away a few feet, stopped, turned around, and barked soundlessly again.

She could see it wanted them to follow. So they did, and soon they came upon a tall cairn of rocks, whereupon the dog scuttled silently away. She spotted a man sitting perched atop the high rock pile, hunched over, resting his chin against his fist. He seemed lost in deep thought.

"Hello!" Lee called out.

The man tweaked his head to look at her, then at the other four. He rose to his feet and, with the same ease as skipping down two stairs, hopped off the towering heap and landed in front of them, making a jangling sound. He wore a strange mechanical suit, a metallic sheath covered in nuts and bolts and tubes enclosing him head to toe. He stood akimbo. "Hello there." Through his faceplate, even his voice sounded metallic.

"Hmm," Percy hmmed. "Most beguiling indeed!"

The man was tall and wide, taller and wider than any of them, and he shined in the afternoon light. Lee couldn't see his eyes through their trapezoid-shaped openings. He had a hinged plate for a mouth, but otherwise his iron face was flat. His suit was made of lots of small parts bolted or hinged together, and around his joints were pistons of various sizes that controlled his motions. Large pipes came out his back facing upwards, like a church organ, and steam came whistling out. There was something unsettling about his mechanical presence.

He stood there, surveying them in detail, until he fixed his sights on Percy. Without warning he jumped like a spring, crossing the distance between them instantly, and grabbed Percy's mustache between his metal fingers.

"I beg your pardon," Percy rumbled. "Release my moustache!"

"I like this ornamental structure at the center of your face. I think I might make me one," the man responded, in an even-paced, mechanical voice, letting go of it.

"I'm Lee. What's your name?"

He looked at her: a noise emanated from behind his empty eye-openings, like whirling cogwheels and levers working at a frenzied pace.

"You know—I have never thought of one. Never had the need to."

"You don't have a name?" She was baffled.

"No." His head made a *WHIRRR* sound. "Should I adopt a title for you to address me by?"

"I should expect so," said Percy.

"But only if you want to," Lee hurried to add. Considering his evident strength, she preferred not to antagonize him.

"It is not important," the man said, after a moment of thought. "I will erase it from my memory as soon as you are gone, since I will have no more need for it."

"But, without a name, how do people know who you are?"

"If they ask, I simply tell them who I am. I am me. But if I keep a name, they would tell me who I am. And I am no one but myself."

"Bien." Óseo snorted.

"Why do you wear that metal suit?" she asked the man, wondering how he looked underneath.

"Suit? I am not wearing a suit. I do not shed my outer layer like people or reptiles. It is very unseemly. I am what I am," he answered proudly.

"Oh, flimflam and gobbledygook. Do you take us for fools?" Percy huffed.

"You do not believe me?"

He sounded offended, Lee thought.

"No, sir, I do not," Percy stated.

The man grabbed on to one hand with the other and proceeded to twist it clean off at the wrist. He held it up; the fingers waved at them. White steam came out the hollow stomp of his wrist. He then put the hand back in place and did the same to his head; with half a twist, he unfastened it from the neck and brought it down to Lee and Percy's height. Now that they were at eye level, she could see into his head through his eyes. He really did have whirling cogwheels and levers, as well as tiny pistons and pumps and pulleys and tubes and other moving bits, like a working colony of mechanical parts.

"By Jove!" Percy was flabbergasted. "Positively smashing. What a marvelous contraption."

The mechanical man screwed his head back on, pretty pleased with himself.

"Who created you?" Percy asked.

"My creator, obviously."

"Who is zat?" Queen Couronne looked at him.

"The Machinesmith." He thumped his chest, making a sound like banging against a metal barrel.

"You know the Machinesmith?" Lee got all keyed up. It meant she was close. "So… you know where he is?"

"Wherever." He pointed toward the horizon, his arm rotating back almost full circle.

"Astounding!" Percy laughed. "How do you work?" He was as excited as a kid on Christmas morning.

"Steam power, naturally. Employed by pneumatic and hydraulic pistons of special design. It is quite ingenious, is i.t.is i..t..is i…t…is it not?" He stuttered, steam whistling in rapid succession out the pipes on his back. "Forgive me. My jaw-plate gets stuck sometimes when I get excited. And I do get excited when explaining myself."

"Ingenious indeed, I heartily agree," Percy said, all wide-eyed.

"I am a great machine. The greatest ever built, no doubt," he added, looking at Lee. He smelled strange, like her old home's boiler room.

"How is it? Being a machine?" she asked.

He stopped to think, his head producing another *WHIRRR.*

"What is your favorite color?"

"Umm, yellow. Sunflower yellow."

"What is you favorite smell?"

She considered it for a moment. "I have two: my bubble bath soap and a candy store. But candy store more."

"What is your favorite sound?"

She'd never thought about it before. It took her a long moment to decide. "I think a lot of water, like the ocean. If that counts. I don't know."

"Well, being a machine means that I do not enjoy things. I only appreciate them."

"How come?"

"Because I have no senses, only sensors. I have no favorite color. No favorite smell. No favorite sound. No favorite anything. I do not prefer any one thing to another. It is useless to do so. I see and hear and smell much better than any of you, without having to bother with things meaning more than what they are. I exist, without having to experience."

She thought what a curious feeling that must be.

"Humph. Yes, yes, I suppose there would be that, wouldn't it?" said Percy.

"Well, I hope you'll be able to, one day," she said.

"Why? I do not 'hope.' I am without hope as I am without despair. I am only what I am. Which is more than I can s.ay f..or..f.o.r..for y.y...ou..you." He sneered, his jaw-plate hinging wide, clanging repeatedly. He stared at her; the mechanisms behind his eyes whirled at a frantic pace. His back pipes shrilled out white-hot steam. Things started clicking and clacking in his head, producing mechanical gargling sounds. It was clear he couldn't stop himself. He tried holding his jaw shut, but it was too late. His cheeks cracked, fracturing his face open like a horrible smile, until it went all the way around and the top half of his head came sliding off, rolling on the ground before coming to a stop in front of them. Its insides were now little more than molten slag, steaming.

"I guess yu *can* laugh yur head off…" Óseo cautiously poked his metal chest, but he remained unmoving. Lee felt sorry for the great machine.

"Godspeed to you, sir," Percy said, and without another word, they went off in the direction he had pointed, toward Wherever.

XIV

Day turned into night. A very bright night. The idea of Wherever was still unclear to Lee, but they came across no one else they could ask about the Machinesmith.

They walked for hours, the scenery slowly changing around them. The trees became sparser, the rocks smaller, the earth bare of any grass or weeds. Eventually, she noticed that her feet were no longer stepping on small pebbles and grains of sand. She was walking on a smooth surface, like black steel. There was nothing else, just empty space, as if they had simply walked off the canvas on which the world was painted.

"Look, up ahead!" Mrs. Adocchiare spotted something. A large, corroded black iron gate, adorned with elaborate curves and twirls, stood between two pillars of crumbling stone, and nothing else. Lee walked around it with care. There was nothing there to see. Curious, she walked back and, with effort, pushed open the gate. It creaked and yawned wide. They passed through it, and as it clanged shut behind them, reverberating loudly through the air, they could see now that they were standing on a faint white-painted trail, which started at the gate and continued out of sight.

The path didn't stay level for long. It twisted and turned and curled and coiled and bulked and bubbled and wound about, but they stuck to it, climbing and sliding their way along.

The glow of the night sky grew brighter. Eventually, they reached the abrupt end of the faded road, at the sharp edge of a precipice. On the other side of the wide rift rose a steep vertical cliff, reaching high above them. Both rock faces dropped deep down, disappearing into bottomless darkness.

"Well, this is grand!" Percy twisted his mouth like he just bit into rotten fruit. "A right chasm that is. May as well be a moat around a castle."

Lee tilted her head back all the way, looking up the cliff. "I think it is."

"Let us find some means of ingress, shall we?" Percy suggested, and the five of them started walking along the edge, hoping to come across an entryway.

"Percy—look at zis!" Queen Couronne called out. Her voice echoed across the void below. The ground dipped where she stood, curving into a narrow tongue-like outgrowth of rock, extending almost to the other cliff. With great care, they walked on it until they reached its slender tip. Lee reached out—the cliff was a few feet away.

"We must head back," Mrs. Adocchiare said.

"No." Lee shook her head, looking up. "This is the way in."

"¡No way!" Óseo waved his skeletal hands. "¿Yu mean yu want tu climb up this thing? That's a really, really, really bad idea, chica."

"Now listen here, old bean, I shall have none of your ne'er-do-well attitude." Percy walked up to stand by her. "I've climbed the icy cliffs of Nanga Parbat myself, whilst on expedition down the Indus River, with little more than ropes and ice-picks. It can be done—believe you me!"

"Mes frères, have you all lost your minds?" Queen Couronne said. "Zat cliff is hundreds of feet high! C'est impossible."

Óseo and Mrs. Adocchiare strongly voiced their agreement. Lee walked to the very point of the rock-tongue and stared down into the abyss. It felt as if it was coming up to greet her. She didn't generally mind heights—she quite liked them, in fact—but the thought of climbing that high and in the dark was petrifying. Nevertheless, that was the way to save her dad, and she would do anything for him. He would for her.

She retreated past the four, who were still busy arguing, then sprinted forward and, before any of them realized what she was doing, leaped off the edge and onto the side of the cliff, grabbing on to its rocks with a concentration of all her might. She didn't wait for their reaction; she started climbing.

She avoided looking down or up; she focused only on her climb, searching for rock formations that she could use to pull herself up or push off of. She could hear the four below had stopped their bickering. After a moment she recognized Percy's grunt as he jumped

on the cliff, followed by Óseo, then Queen Couronne, and finally Mrs. Adocchiare.

Percy, climbing with unexpected nimbleness, appeared at her side within an instant. They scaled the steep crag with the rest following at different paces, Queen Couronne being the slowest, having to climb in a gown and her head in a jar. They climbed high enough that when Lee eventually peeked down, despite her best efforts not to, all she could see was darkness.

She turned her attention to finding the next outcrop to grab onto when the rock beneath her feet gave way. She plummeted past Percy and Óseo and Mrs. Adocchiare and Queen Couronne, screaming wildly—until her bag snagged on a jutting rock, stopping her fall with a forceful jerk and bashing her against the cliff. Some apples and a few of her brushes tumbled into the abyss. Her vision blurred, turning dim around the edges. She dug her fingers into the rockface as best she could. Her muscles shook from head to toe.

"¿Niña, are yu all right?" Óseo called out.

She wanted to nod but didn't dare move.

Percy climbed down beside her and supported her against the cliff. "You gave us quite the scare."

"I'm okay," she said, still woozy. She noticed now that her knees were scraped, staining her pajamas with glistening scarlet.

"Very well, enough faffing about then. Come, there's work to be done. Shipshape and Bristol fashion!" Percy tried to sound unruffled. They resumed their climb. Eventually, finally, mercifully, they reached the top. She felt triumphant.

Atop the cliff stood a tall, austere castle. Not the kind with pointed turrets and fluttering banners: it was made up entirely of soaring black stone walls and towers. It was completely windowless, and at its entrance stood a pair of great wooden doors clutched by rusted ironwork, impenetrable.

There was no bell to ring or handles to pull. Just two metal hands, one on each door, sculpted as if reaching out. One faced down and had a hinge at the wrist. The other faced up, holding a large metal orb. Lee tried picking it up, but it was too heavy. With Óseo's help she managed to free it, and, intuitively, pushed it up into the other hand, where it snapped into place. Clearly, the doorknocker.

Pulling the hand down with both of hers, she banged the orb against the door. It released a deafening roar, filling the still night air. The castle was silent. She approached to pull on the hand again, when the massive doors opened with a deep groan. After a moment's hesitation, they all walked in. The doors closed behind them—not with a loud slam, as she expected, but with a whisper.

The castle had no courtyard. At the farthest corner of its black walls stood a fortified keep, with a single wide, tall tower. At the top of the tower was a single window, facing out over the abyss, the only window in the entire castle. The light was on.

The interior of the keep was spacious and dark. It had no tapestries, no paintings, no furniture, no statues, no decorations of any kind. Nothing but a giant chandelier, hanging from the immensely tall ceiling of the entrance hall. Its crystals were tear-shaped, casting a glow that made the walls look like they were crying light. Queen Couronne took the opportunity to preen herself. She straightened her jar, fastening its straps under her shoulders, then brushed off and readjusted her dress. When she was done and ready, she nodded and they moved on.

The hall continued into a long, dusty corridor, framed by decayed support beams and crumbling mortar. What little light there was came from candle holders hanging on the walls, the wicks dangling fatigued over the melted edges of the candles. They flickered as the five of them walked by.

The corridor led into a second hall, similarly empty. At its other end was a broad staircase spiraling up to the tower. They climbed the stone steps, uneasy. When they finally reached the top, they found the narrow window they had spotted earlier. It was pitch black outside, even though dawn should have already arrived.

"Zere is somezing… inquiétant about zis place," Queen Couronne whispered.

"Indeed, madam. Gives me the jimjams, it does. Best we be prudent," Percy said.

Dust made its way up Lee's nose, goading an abrupt sneeze.

"Gesundheit! You know, it's a well-documented fact that when someone sneezes that loud an angel explodes." The voice echoed off the stone walls. Lee peered into the darkness, looking for its source. A light turned on and a man appeared, tall and lean, with slicked-back silver hair, except for one long strand dangling by his temple. He was wearing goggles that pressed into his face, pushing his eyebrows into folds on top of them. Also wearing a long, dirtied white lab coat that reached below his knees, he completed his comical appearance with long, black rubber gloves that were cracked and torn at their tips, revealing yellowing fingers.

"You're the Machinesmith!" Lee understood, jumping with excitement.

"Indeed I am, my pet. Machinesmith, inventor, engineer, scientist. Auric Reuben, at your service. Call me Auric." He smiled.

"Oh, how wonderful," Mrs. Adocchiare said. "We've come a very long way in search of you."

"I should hope so. I certainly didn't want it to be all that easy." He smiled at Lee through his goggles. "Who are you, and why do you seek me?"

"I'm Lee," she answered. "And these are my friends: Percy, Mrs. Adocchiare, Queen Couronne, and Óseo. We've come to you for help."

His buggy eyes looked thoughtful for a minute. "I see. Well, then, I can't do much for you here in the entryway. We'll need to make use of my laboratory. Follow me."

He led the way, cocking his head to the side every so often in quick ticks to release small creaks from his neck. They followed him into a large open space, which was clearly an elaborate laboratory. Giant machines of all kinds thrummed and pulsated. Lit-up diodes buzzed and crackled. Large gauges shook and jittered. Beakers and test tubes fizzed and bubbled. Auric's lab was a bustle of animated commotion. Lee looked around inquisitively.

"Quite a hodgepodge of apparatuses you have here. I can see why they call you the Machinesmith," said Percy.

"Certainly!" he boasted. "Be careful not to touch anything, my pet," he called over to Lee, who was about to fidget with some gadget resting on a table. "Some of the things here might be dangerous even if they don't look it, yes?" She nodded, though she didn't like being called "pet."

"My latest project has been inventing a perpetuum mobile machine. I've almost got it," he said, scurrying to the other end of his lab in a mad frenzy. "Actually, I've had my results for a long time, but I don't yet know how I'm to arrive at them!"

He pulled on a curtain, revealing a display of strange machines in various stages of construction. He picked one off its rack, a helmet resting on some fabric and wires. "This is my natatory machine!" He put on the helmet, then a thick life vest. The helmet had hinged pedals coming out the top, like giant rabbit ears, connected to wires that ran though a series of metal rings down the vest, ending in two handles. He pulled on them, operating the pedals on the helmet. "I got the idea from microbes—they swim using their antennae!"

"What a rigmarole!" Percy laughed. "Would it not simply be easier to perform the natural motions of swimming?"

Auric blinked through his goggles. "That's entirely beside the point. What's important is that now there's a machine for it."

"Ha!" Percy bellied another laugh. "Spoken like a true inventor, indeed."

"Yes," Auric agreed. "While half of my brain is trying to translate my thought into working machines, the other half is already busy thinking up new ones." He grinned like a child.

"C'est bon," Queen Couronne said, aloofly polite.

"Sí—on the left side of his brain nothing is right, and on the right side nothing is left," Óseo whispered so only Lee could hear. She giggled. She was eager to ask Auric about finding her father, but just as she was about to ask him, he rolled out another machine from the display. This one much bigger and bulkier, crowded with gears and wires and cords and coils. "Observe this!" he gestured. "This is my perambulation machine."

He slipped into what reminded her of a sleeping bag, buttoning it tightly all the way up to his chest. It hung like a cocoon from a metal fork mounted onto a steel frame, and when he turned two crank handles connected to pulleys, like bike pedals for his hands, two long limbs pivoted down to the ground, hoisting him up in the air. He walked around in the device, the racket of rotating gears and squeaking hinges so loud that she had to stick her fingers in her ears.

"Ingeniously constructed, sir! But must that contraption produce such infernal ruckus?" Percy raised his voice over the noise.

"Well, I do have some kinks to work out, I know…" Auric reluctantly admitted, setting it down.

"Hmm. I expect so." Queen Couronne sniffed.

"But why do you build machines that do what people can already do anyway? Wouldn't it be better to build machines that do other things instead?" Lee questioned.

He looked at her, cocking his head to the side again to release another crackle. He pulled his goggles on top of his head. His eyes were like beads—small, round, and shiny pale blue. "What can be more useful than a natatory machine or a perambulation machine? And I've also invented, so you know, a soporific machine, which makes you sleep, a deipnosophist machine, which makes you talk, an orthostatic machine, which makes you stand, and a decumbenting machine, which makes you lie down. That's why I'm the Machinesmith!" He tilted his chin up.

"But… but these are all things everybody can do. Nobody needs a machine for any of that."

"What do you mean? Of course they do!" Auric was offended. "With my machines they'd perform these actions much better," he stated with authority. With that, he turned around and galloped over to a buzzing machine, fitfully pulling on several giant switches and tapping to check its gauges.

She tugged at Óseo's sleeve, informing him, without saying a word, that she didn't think much of Auric.

Óseo giggled. He found his kookiness endearing.

Auric finished playing with his machine and skipped back over. "So—now you know all about me. Tell me why you've come to me for help."

She told him. It took her a long time, but Auric listened very carefully, taking in every detail.

"That's an incredible story," he said after a few moments of silence. "A little live girl, travelling the afterworlds in search of her father, in the company of four dead friends." His eyes sparkled with glee. He paused, thinking it over some more. "Well, it just goes to show—even little girls have skeletons in their closet!" He chuckled at Óseo, thinking the joke original.

"Can you help me find Wherever? That's where my dad is." She hoped that, despite his nuttiness, he'd be able to.

The grin across his face spread even wider. "Oh, I believe I can. I have a pretty good idea where it is."

"Really?" She could feel her heartbeat through her entire body.

"Marvelous!" Percy said.

Auric nodded and waved his hand in eager motions for them to follow, leading them to the farthermost end of his gigantic lab. It was much quieter there, without the thrumming and pulsating and buzzing machines. There was only a fireplace in the castle's black brick wall. The fire was small, little flames bopping and hissing atop the firewood. There was nothing else in that corner of the lab—except a large sphere, hovering in the air at Lee's height.

"What in the name of heaven!" Percy's jaw dropped, pulling his mustache after it.

The sphere was completely black, not even the slightest reflection of light on it. It was perfectly round, and perfectly silent, and perfectly dark.

"What... what is it?" she asked.

"Can't you see it's a door, my pet?" Auric scoffed. "What—all doors have to be flat rectangles? Do people come in flat shapes? Is the Earth flat? No, it's not, is it? It's round. So why can't a door be round?"

"Door to where?"

"Wherever. It's the next world. The last, as far as I can tell. It seems to be more of an abstract place than an actual location. My tests have so far proven inconclusive."

She stared at the black orb, floating inches from her face. It was exactly like staring into the back of her closet. The others all gaped at it, wordlessly.

"How'd you get it in here?" she wondered.

Auric shook his head. "I didn't. It's as old and infinite as time itself. I found it here. I built my lab around the sphere, and I built this fortress around the lab."

"How come?"

Auric took a long, deep breath, then released it as a long, deep sigh. "I was a little boy once, just like you. And just like you, I wandered one day into the darkness. Mine wasn't in the back of my closet, though. It was in our basement. I was the only one of my brothers not afraid to go down there. So, of course, I'd sneak down there to play whenever I didn't want to share my toys… and then I started noticing the darkness, at the very back of the basement. And one night I walked through it, only to discover, then, that I couldn't get back. I remember yelling for my parents, so hard and for so long that my throat stopped producing sound. I was stuck there, alone in the dark. So I explored the void, and eventually I found my way here."

"So you're alive, like me? And you grew up here, all alone?" Lee said. "I'm so sorry."

"You've been sequestered here since childhood?" Percy echoed.

"So long ago now…" Auric remained frozen, staring into the air.

It was the worst possible thing she could ever imagine.

"And you've been trying all this time to pass through the sphere? To get home?" she asked.

He gave her half a nod, mumbling to himself. Thinking, he started pacing the length and breadth of the fireplace area, backward and forward, backward and forward, the tip of his face twitching.

"You poor, poor thing," Mrs. Adocchiare said.

An angry glare flickered across his face for a fraction of a second. He didn't care for their pity.

"True, I haven't been able to get through the door, so far. But, as luck would have it, I do have a way of helping all of you. It's my greatest invention!" He assumed a proud smile. "Would you like to see it?"

"But of course!" Percy said.

"Very much indeed!" Queen Couronne said.

Lee nodded fervently, bathed in pure joy. She was about to see her dad again. She couldn't reach Auric's machine fast enough.

"It's all the way downstairs, though. You can leave your bag here, if you want." He pointed to a table with some empty space left on it between thrown-about springs and hinges. She put her bag down, pocketing an apple for later, and rushed down the long flight of stairs ahead of the others.

They followed the staircase back to the hallway, where they came in. She noticed for the first time that it also continued downward. Auric motioned them to follow. The stairway ended at a dimly lit corridor leading to a small, dark, round chamber.

"Stay close against the walls," Auric said, standing by the doorway holding onto a large switch. "We need as much clear space in the center of the room for this to work."

They spread out, standing back as far as they could, and Auric threw the switch. There was a quick rumble behind them, from inside the walls, and then, almost instantly, metal chains dropped around them from above, tightening and pressing them against the wall before any of them could react.

"Wha—what is the meaning of this?" Percy yelled out.

Auric stepped into the room, smirking. "Surpriiiiise!"

"Why, you scoundrel! What do you want of us?" Percy growled at him.

Auric crossed his arms, bursting with smugness. He looked at the five of them held against the wall, struggling to escape the chains. "Nothing. What would you have that I need? I just want you to stay here, with me. As my guests," he said, matter-of-factly.

"Mon dieu! I knew you spoke utter nonsense wiz utter confidence, but I did not zink you are malicious," Queen Couronne said with as much contempt as she could muster.

He walked up to her, leaned in close, and tapped on her jar, right in front of her face. *Tink-tink.*

"My word! Such ghastly behavior. We thought you a friend, man. Have you no shame? Release us," Percy growled again.

He tilted his head at Percy, releasing a snap from his neck. He shook his head, still grinning, like a cheeky little boy refusing to clean his room.

"Listen, Auric," Óseo said, trying to sound compassionate. "I understand yu are angry for being stuck here for so long. I know it's not fair. Trust me, I know how it is tu lose everything yu—"

"No you *don't!*" Auric screamed, stomping his feet. "You don't know anything. You can't know what it's like, being all alone for a hundred years!"

"¿Hundred?" Óseo was taken by surprise. "¿Yur not alive anymore, are yu?"

Auric glared again. "No. I'm not. I grew up here, I grew old here, and I died here. And now—now I'm a wraith. You know what that is? It's like a ghost. I'm too dead to go back, but I'm not dead enough to move on. I can't get to Wherever. So I'm just stuck here, in between, in this stupid castle. That's not how it's supposed to be. It's not fair!" His eyes shone bright with madness.

"I don't care!" Lee screamed furiously. "You're a monster. Let us go!"

"Oh, no." He shook his head. "I'm just misunderstood. I'm miserable, you see," he said in a pitiful, mocking voice.

"Monsters are always miserable. That's why they're monsters," Mrs. Adocchiare said.

Auric walked by her, ignoring her. He stopped in front of Lee, leaning so close that their noses almost touched. "I've been thinking."

"About what?" She stared back at him, defiant.

"When you were telling me your story, and how you managed to travel from world to world, it got me thinking. And I realized something." He waited.

"What?" she asked, reluctantly.

"I realized that you were right, and I was wrong. Isn't that brave of me to admit?"

She said nothing.

"For more than a century now, I've been trying, and failing, to pass through the darkness that keeps me trapped here. And then you come, with your little kiddie paints and brushes, and move through it like there was nothing to it. I've been going at it all wrong, you see? Art is the key, not science. The heart, not the mind."

"You've clearly lost the former and make no use of the latter, you ragamuffin!" Percy barked at him.

"Oh, you're still angry over the whole locking-you-up-in-chains business, aren't you? I'm sorry," he offered with demented sincerity. "I'm afraid it was necessary. And necessity is the mother of invention, you know."

Lee looked at Percy; he looked worried. Very worried.

"Let the girl go, Auric," Óseo said. "The rest of us will stay here with yu."

Auric glanced at him, scornful. "You? Who cares about you? You're dead. Lee's the one I want—she's going to help me out of here. And if not, she'll stay here, with me, forever."

Auric scared her, but as much as she was scared *of* him, she was much more scared *by* him; he was everything she was afraid of becoming. "No way! I'm not going to stay with you for a minute. Let us all go, right now," she yelled at him with a conviction that surprised them both.

"Oh, but you will be, my pet. Just you and me, together, for infinite infinities…."

"I'd rather die than stay here with you."

"Be careful what you wish for, my pet. If you really leave me with no other choice, you'll get your wish. I mean…" He slicked back his dangling strand of hair and wetted his lips with a tongue as yellow and cracked as the tips of his fingers. "I'd hate to, but it's not like

221

it hasn't happened before. Every good scientist goes through a process of trial and error."

"What do you mean?" she asked, suspicious.

"What—you think you're the first little girl to discover a secret passageway to a hidden world? Pfft. Please." He snickered, curling his lip. "There were others before you. Many others. They all stumbled into the darkness—through a hole in the ground or inside their wardrobe or down in their basement or up in their attic or under their bed—they all eventually found their way to my castle. And they all just wanted to go home. Not one of them wanted to help me get out or to stay here with me. Those selfish brats!"

She looked deep into his beady, wild eyes, and realized, to her mounting horror, that he was telling the truth. She wasn't the first. Other kids had found their way into the darkness. Other kids had reached the castle before her. And she knew, with certainty, that none of them had ever made it out.

Percy pushed against the chains running across his chest. They didn't give, even in the slightest. "You deranged madman!"

Mrs. Adocchiare clucked her tongue, like a disappointed grandmother. "You obviously suffer from some fevered dementia, Auric. Such a pity. But I'm sure that if we put our minds to it, together we can figure out a way to help you. You just need to have a little faith."

Auric walked up to her. He leaned in, like he did with Queen Couronne and Lee, but Mrs. Adocchiare kept her kind expression. He stared into her eyes, noticing her left one. He slowly reached for it. She winced, trying to tilt her head away, but his yellow-stained fingers found it, and, with a loud, wet "*POP*," plucked it out of place.

"What are you doing? Leave her be!" Queen Couronne snarled.

He pulled his goggles down and held up Mrs. Adocchiare's eyeball, examining it. He sniggered, pulled the goggles back up, and dropped it on the ground. Before it could roll away, he stepped on it, gradually, splattering it against the black stone. It produced a sickening sound, crunchy and wet, like a cracking egg.

Mrs. Adocchiare let out a terrible wail—Lee couldn't tell if it was more in agony or in sorrow. Auric screeched with laughter.

"You fiend!" Percy bellowed.

"¡Bastardo!" Óseo yelled.

She looked over at Mrs. Adocchiare, still sobbing. Then at Auric. Shock and fear and rage roiled in her all at once. "You *are* dead—the boy inside of you died a long time ago!" she screamed at him. "And I'll never stay with you. Ever!"

Auric's face quickly turned from grinning to crimson red, veins pressing out his forehead like lightning bolts. His whole frame panted, seething, but she stared him straight in the eye. He slapped her, hard. After a moment, she was able to focus. She turned her head back to him. The coppery taste of blood filled the corner of her mouth. He face burned with pain. Tears filled her eyes. But she refused to cry.

"You miserable cur!" Percy growled, rattling his chain. "How dare you lay your hand on a child!"

"¡Esto colma la medida! ¡Yu leave her alone, yu…!" Óseo spitted through gnashing teeth.

Queen Couronne said something also, but Lee couldn't hear it. "I hate you! I'll always hate you. I'll hate you forever," she vowed.

Auric recomposed himself. "Yes, you will at first, no doubt. You will despise me. But not forever. You don't know what forever means. You have no idea. In due course, despite yourself, you will come to accept me as fact. And with only me for companionship, eventually you will come to love me, my pet. When you can no longer even remember why you hate me." He turned and walked out of the room.

"Know this, knave—if any harm befalls the girl I shall hold you accountable! You hear me?" Percy called after him, his voice echoing down the narrow corridor. But Auric was already gone.

"Mrs. Adocchiare? Are you all right?" Lee asked.

"Never mind me, dear. I'll be just fine," Mrs. Adocchiare said.

Lee was not convinced. "I'm so sorry."

"Oh, tush," Mrs. Adocchiare said. "You mustn't blame yourself—he has a scorpion's tale for a tongue, that one. We were all fooled."

Lee hung her head, saying nothing. It wasn't important anymore. It was too late.

XV

They hung from their shackles for a long time, pressed tightly against the chamber wall. Lee couldn't tell how long. She was lost in thought, downcast and downhearted. Percy and Óseo at first spent some time debating and planning their escape, but eventually, they realized, it was a futile effort. They had no room to move to do anything about it.

Hours passed. Beyond the dungeon there was no sound, and little light came in from the candles in the corridor.

Lee looked at Mrs. Adocchiare and at Queen Couronne and at Óseo and at Percy. Percy looked back apologetically, as if he let her, and the rest of them, down. His sigh was heavy. "I fear our quest has run its course, my friends." There was sadness and exhausted resignation in his voice, which she had never heard before.

"Have faith, Percy," Mrs. Adocchiare said, trying her best to smile through one eye. "And patience. Patience is a virtue. We'll find a way out, in time."

Percy looked down at the black floor, almost shamefully. "I'm afraid that's quite impossible, dear madam." His great white mustache and his great white eyebrows wilted down his round face.

Seeing him like this broke Lee's heart. Percy had been her steady rock, the one to give her courage when she faltered. If even he admitted defeat, the situation truly was hopeless. "I'm sorry," she said.

"What on Earth for, child?" He looked up.

"I disappointed you. All of you. And my dad." The tears came down now. She had gotten so close. But she failed. She would never see him again. Never see her mother. Or brother. She failed them all.

"Au contraire, ma chèrie." Queen Couronne tilted her head in her jar. "We are what we most repeatedly do—and zroughout our many trials and tribulations, you have shown nozing but courage again and again. You are a very brave girl, and we are all proud of you, no matter what happens."

"I'm sure your father is very proud of you as well," Mrs. Adocchiare agreed.

Lee listened, while observing Percy observing the two women; she could see they reignited something in him. It slowly spread across his face, raising his mustache back up to its prideful place. "By golly, you're right! Listen here, young lady—I'll admit, the situation seems dire. But where hope is coldest, and despair most fits—that is when we must call upon our utmost fortitude."

She sniffed her tears away and nodded. He was right. This was far from over. There was no way that

Auric, Machinesmith or not, was going to stop her from finding her dad. An idea struck her. She wriggled under her chains, trying to free her right hand. The metal links chafed painfully against her skin. But she didn't stop, not until she managed to move her hand farther to the side, if ever so slightly. She struggled to bend sideways to reach her pocket, squirming in the rigid tight space between iron and stone, until she managed to send her fingertips into it, carefully pulling out the apple she took with her earlier. It was green.

She let it drop by her feet, which stood free beneath the chains, and looked at Óseo; he was across from her. She thought back to the small village in the middle of Nowhere and their game of Stiltball, and how she managed to beat him.

She took careful aim, and put all her strength into one, powerful kick. The apple hurtled at Óseo, hitting him dead center in the chest bone, smashing him. He came collapsing down out of his chains, dispersing his white bones across the black chamber floor. His head, still in his hat, landed upside-down.

"¡Caramba!"

"Óseo, can you move your arm?" She said.

"I think so, sí."

His arm remained intact, along with part of his ribcage, under his shiny blue shirt. He concentrated, and his hand, resting palm-down on the floor, fidgeted— his fingers arched to clutch the small depressions in the stones, and the arm heaved itself forward across the ground, dragging the rest of him behind. She didn't have to explain her plan; Óseo's arm and torso inched toward the doorway. He used the arm to push the torso up, like a car jack, then swung it to grab onto the large switch above. He pulled on it, and slowly, reluctantly, the handle arched downward. When it reached the switchplate, as quickly as the chains had tightened around them, they were yanked off, disappearing back into the walls. They were free.

"Good show, old bean! Good show!" Percy cheered.

"I wasn't sure I could do it, I'm feeling very scattered right now, je je je."

Mrs. Adocchiare shuffled across the floor to Óseo and joined Lee, Percy, and Queen Couronne in putting him back together. They were done in a matter of moments.

"Voilà!" Queen Couronne said.

"Gracias." Óseo moved his limbs about, making sure all was in working order.

"Lee, you've proven your valor and ingenuity yet again. Bravo!" Percy exalted.

She smiled widely.

"¡Sí, niña. Yu did good." Óseo smiled back. "¿What du yu say we go get yur paints back from that lunatic and go find yur father?"

She nodded.

"¡Ándale!"

The five of them edged up the staircase toward Auric's lab, careful not to raise a sound. Soon enough they found him, crouching over a makeshift easel by the fireplace, one of Lee's canvases propped up against it. The fire threw a ghastly light on his face, revealing a terrible mask of rabid expression. She couldn't quite make out what he was painting, but she could tell it was little more than a jumble of shapes and colors. And he was using up what little paints she had left.

They crept up behind him, blocking his way to his machines, until they were only a few yards away. "Allez!" Queen Couronne called out, and they rushed toward him.

"Bounder! Your moment of reckoning is at hand," Percy yelled. But before they could reach him, he streaked toward the fireplace with Lee's bag of supplies and dangled it above the fire. They stopped in their tracks.

"Ah-ah-ah!" He held out his finger, waving it back and forth like a metronome.

"Give me back my bag," she screamed at him.

He kept it above the fire. "Listen—I admit, I may have been a tad rash, locking you and your friends up like that. But what other choice did I have? Now, I seem to be experiencing some difficulty creating a painting here. I'm not much of an artist… so what do you say we let bygones be bygones, and you show me how to do it, how to travel through the darkness? Then I'll help all of you get to Wherever, or wherever else. Promise!" His eyes darted maniacally between them.

"No. It won't work for you," she said, knowing she was right.

"Then you make it work for me!" Auric yelled, his voice cracking.

She stared him down.

"Well, nevermind—with my brainpower and your talent, we can have full control over everything around us. This can be our perfect world."

"No, thanks. I prefer the real world," she said.

"The real world is for those who can't imagine a better one. The real world is where your parents abandon you," he spewed, a crazed expression overcoming him.

"Shut up!" she yelled back. "You can just go to hell!"

"Why, you stiff-necked little girl. If I can't leave here, you won't either." He dropped the bag into the fire, releasing a shower of sparks out into the room.

She watched helplessly as it burned away, the canvases eaten by hissing flames. Pure horror washed over her, followed by pure panic. "*No. No!*"

"My god, what have you done, villain?" Percy cried out.

Auric stomped his foot, waving his finger wildly. "If I can't, you can't. I told you so!"

"You selfish little brat," Percy growled.

Auric launched himself snarling at Percy. Percy raised his arms instinctively, but Auric's assault was a ruse; he knocked him and Queen Couronne down to the ground, dashing for his machines. But before he could take one from the display, Percy jumped him from behind, swiveling him away into a table cluttered with parts. Auric picked up a metal rod with a wide, sharp-toothed cogwheel at its end, and ran at Percy, swinging wildly. Percy sprang out of the way right as Auric's weapon smashed into one of the machines behind him, shattering it to bits.

Auric didn't seem to care—he pressed the attack, cutting through the air with whistles. Lee looked around frantically. She picked up a poker from the fireplace and threw it to Percy. "Percy!" He grabbed it just in time to deflect Auric's blow. He brandished the poker like a sword. "Have at you, you dastardly rogue!"

The two clashed in a succession of swinging and jabbing, lunging and parrying, their weapons spitting sparks whenever they collided. Auric had the upper hand; he was much taller than Percy and his reach much longer, and he knew the lay of the lab. He kept Percy on the defensive, steering him backwards into as many obstacles as he could. But Percy wielded his poker with skill, managing to fend off Auric's repeated assaults.

Their battle raged across the lab, smashing every item in their path. Auric kept swinging ferociously, and Percy kept swashbuckling—ducking under things and jumping on top of things and rolling over things. They spilled out into the small hallway with the window. There wasn't much room there for Percy to maneuver, which was exactly what Auric intended. He blocked Percy's dodging, striking him atop the head. He then lunged at him, forcing Percy against the window. Still reeling from the powerful blow, Percy was slowly being pushed out the window. His feet rose off the ground, his head and shoulders tilting over the window ledge. Auric hunched over him, leering, pressing the sharp cogwheel to his throat, about to send him over, when Queen Couronne leaped at Auric's feet, picked them up from under him, and flipped him over Percy and out the tower window, down to the abyss below. He fell screaming, and then the screaming faded into nothing.

"Kind thanks, madam. I am forever in your debt," Percy panted, pulling himself back down. "If not for you, it'd have been curtains for me."

Queen Couronne seemed indifferent to his gratitude. "Zat is quite all right, Percy. *Someone* had to take care of zat menace." And with that she turned around and walked back into the lab. Percy followed, chuckling.

They stepped over the ruins of the Machinesmith's machines, reaching the fireplace at the far corner of the lab. The fire was mostly out now, a smoldering pile resting on top. Lee used a poker to drag her bag out. All but one of her canvases had burnt to a crisp, and even that one was charred around most of the edges. Tears came streaming down her trembling chin. "It's not fair...." She hated to be crying again, but she couldn't help it. It was too late to bring her father back.

"Hush, my dear... I know. I know," Mrs. Adocchiare said, in her gentle, kindhearted way, hugging her tightly. "But sometimes things are neither fair nor unfair. Sometimes things are just... life. Death as well."

She understood, reluctantly. Mrs. Adocchiare used a finger to wipe the tears from her eyes. "I don't know what to do now. I can't find my dad anymore. And I can't get back home."

"Yu can still paint on this canvas, more or less, no?" Óseo said, holding up the half-burnt thing. Her paint tubes, almost empty, were scattered around the easel.

She gave an unsure nod. "I guess… but, there's only one. I had enough to get all of us to Wherever, and now there's only one left…."

"Listen, niña—forget Wherever. Use it tu get back home. Yur mother must be worried sick."

Unhappily, she agreed. She thought of her mom and Ron. She didn't know how much time had passed, or if they knew she was even gone. They lost her dad just as she had. She couldn't put them through losing her, as well.

She looked at Óseo. His skull face looked back with a caring expression.

"Óseo?"

"¿Sí…?"

"You never told me how you got to the room where I met you. Can you tell me now? Please?"

He looked at her, considering, and groaned. A lone, long, deep groan. "Bien. Yu are right." She looked at Percy, Mrs. Adocchiare, and Queen Couronne. They'd heard the story before. Their sad faces confirmed it.

"I come from España, as yu know. From the coast near Cádiz. I was a poor fisherman, fishing peces and camarónes in my little boat. I made a meager living, but it was enough tu support me and my wife, so we were happy. Her name was Adelina…" He paused, remembering. "She was pregnant with our first child when I went out tu sea one day, never tu return tu her. I drowned. And all the little fishes nibbled on me, picked me clean. And that is how I came tu be as yu know me, niña."

Óseo's sorrow sat like a weight on her chest. Of all their stories, his was the saddest. He never had the chance to say goodbye to his wife. And worse, he never even got to say hello to his child. She looked into his eyes and saw the ache in them, and she knew then what she had to do.

She took the partially burnt canvas, put it up on Auric's easel, mixed together what paints she could, and started painting. The four of them thought she was painting her way back home, she knew. But she wasn't. Instead, she painted a small dinghy, sailing across a foaming sea. When she was done, she joined the others sitting on the floor. There was nothing to do but wait now. The fireplace still radiated warmth, and exhaustion took over. She fell asleep.

XVI

Lee slowly woke up to the sound of gentle waves sloshing about. She found herself in a small room, lit by the soft yellow of a lazy morning sun. She sat up and looked around, her feet releasing a creak from the floorboards as they touched down; the room had no furniture, save for the cot she was on and a narrow, unpainted wooden table by the adjacent wall.

The sound of another wave caught her attention, and she promptly stood up. The room had one large window, with a blue-green frame, and a door of the same rich color hung open beside it.

In four steps she crossed the room and stepped outside, finding herself on a white patio that reflected the sun in blinding glow. A winding staircase of white-coated brick led down toward a base of rocks, where the waves swayed timidly back and forth. The room, she could now see, was the entirety of a small home, perched atop a cliff that the waves had carved out. It overlooked the clear blue ocean, which extended to the horizon, where it kissed the brilliant sky, mirroring its white clouds.

She walked down toward the cove. The sea was crystal clear, all the way to the bottom where colorful schools of fish swam about. At the end of the cove was a small marina, and one small dinghy, tied to a small pier, swaying gently atop the froth of the waves. It was crudely patched in several spots with thin boards, and a fishing net was strung across it to dry in the sun.

"¿What did yu du, niña?" Óseo's voice came from behind. She turned around, smiling sheepishly, when she saw the skeleton standing in front of her. Only it wasn't a skeleton at all; it was a man, smiling at her. He was young, and handsome, and had a perfect, shining smile. His white pants were clean again, as was his shiny blue short-sleeve button shirt. He pulled up the rim of his straw hat, no longer crumpled, and winked at her, with eyes as blue as the ocean by their feet.

"Óseo?" A woman's voice surprised them both.

The woman stood at a distance, hesitating. She held the hand of a little girl. The two of them looked alike, both raven-haired and olive-skinned and very beautiful. Óseo's blue eyes widened.

"Adelina…"

She ran to him and jumped into his arms, her bare feet lifting off the ground. They held each other tight, burying their faces in each other's necks.

When he opened his eyes again, he saw the little girl, still at a distance, still uncertain. He put Adelina down and kneeled to her height. They stared at each other, father and daughter, strangers, meeting for the first time.

"Elena," Adelina told him her name.

"Elena," he whispered it back, as if the very sound of her name filled him with wonderment and joy.

A spark of recognition lit up the little girl's eyes. Óseo was no longer just a strange man. She ran to her papa. He hugged her, as strong and as warm as a man can.

Lee walked away, giving them some time alone. She took off her bootie slippers and strolled down to the water. Grains of sand sneaked between her toes, and when she walked into the perfectly warm ocean, her feet prickled from the seashells and pebbles sprinkled across the surf line. She breathed in the crisp, salty air, and gazed at the horizon. The sea and the sky melted into each other, one continuous blue.

She knew, then, what the dead dreamt about. Óseo dreamt of his family, as they dreamt of him. And she was able to paint those dreams together, the same way she was able to travel through the darkness. She thought of her father, and of how desperately she wanted to see him again. But in the end, she had been left with only one canvas, and she had a choice to make. She made the right one. She hoped that, wherever he was, her dad was dreaming of her, too.

Óseo walked up beside her, the waves caressing their bare feet, and stared with her out into the distance.

"Yu gave up finding yur father for me."

She nodded.

"¿Why?"

237

She kept quiet for a long moment. "Because. Because… I can paint my dad. When I close my eyes, I can see him. I remember him. I wanted you and Elena to have that, too."

Óseo looked at her. A single tear edged down one of his ocean-blue eyes.

"Thank yu, niña."

XVII

They both woke up, together. They were back in the castle, in the lab, resting against the corner of the black wall, facing each other. Óseo's tear rolled down his empty eye socket.

The others were already awake, and having looked at Lee's painting, understood what had taken place. They gazed at her, with great sadness and great pride.

Mrs. Adocchiare then busied herself creating a makeshift eyepatch from a pair of goggles she found, wearing them diagonally across her head so that one capped lens covered her eye while the other rested atop her head. She waddled over to the rest of them, standing by the hovering dark sphere. They hadn't a clue what to do next. Percy reached out to touch it; his hand landed on solid black, like a giant floating marble.

Lee walked up close to the sphere, realizing, but not caring, that she was barefoot. She stared at it. For a second she thought she could see deeper into it. She concentrated, staring harder. Slowly, the sphere grew deeper and darker, until it swelled into a vast, endless darkness. She cautiously reached out to touch it—its surface was smooth and warm, like melted chocolate. She pressed gently against it; her hand sunk in, disappearing up to the wrist. It was like pushing through fog.

A hand grabbed her by the hair. Auric pulled back her head, pressing a jagged piece of machine against her stretched throat. He had snuck up on them while they were engrossed in the sphere. His appearance was gruesome, a sickening mangle of flesh and bone.

"So, I had some more time to think, climbing all the way back up here," he said, calmly, his lips curled into a sinister grin. The others wanted to rush to her aid, but didn't dare with the sharp piece of metal held to her throat. "And then it suddenly occurred to me— the answer isn't in painting at all. It's in you, my pet. You see, it's not your paintings that allow you to travel through the darkness; it's your painting. It's your ability to create what you imagine."

It dawned on her that, as mad as Auric was, he was right. It was never really painting her father that made her travel through the darkness; it was imagining him while she did. Just as she had imagined Mrs. Adocchiare's bird. Just as she had imagined Óseo's wife and daughter. In the darkness, by imagining them, she had made them real.

"Now, my pet, you're going to help me get to Wherever." He pulled on her hair hard, jerking her head. "If you don't, I'll slit your throat right here and now. You wouldn't want to die here and become a wraith like me, and wander this land forever and ever, now would you?"

"You craven!" Percy yelled.

She nodded, with what little leeway Auric left her to move her head. It felt like her scalp was being ripped off.

"Good girl." He smirked. He slowly dragged her backward toward the sphere. The darkness expanded and engulfed them both. Soon, they were swallowed up in absolute black.

"You can let go of me now," she said, boldly. Her plan depended on it. He released her hair but held on tightly to her hand. They walked through the cold void, neither of them able to see anything—not what they were walking on, not even each other—everything was pitch black. But she could feel him, his firm grasp chafing her wrist.

"So now what, my pet? How does this work? Do we walk over there?" he asked.

"I'm not your pet—and you're not going *anywhere*," she answered him, kicking with all her strength at where she hoped was his knee. She hit something that snapped, and Auric let out a grisly howl of pain. His grip loosened a bit, just enough, and in one breathless spurt she pried her hand out of his and started running through the dark, blindly.

"You little brat. I knew you couldn't be trusted!" he screamed. "When I catch you, I'm going to—"

But she wasn't listening. She was desperately looking for a way out. She forced herself to ignore him, to clear her mind, to focus on the others. Ahead of her a round patch of darkness slowly began to dissipate, and she could start to make out their familiar shapes. She raced toward them as fast as she could.

Auric was chasing her close behind—she couldn't see him, but she could hear him screaming. She put all her strength into a mad dash for the round breach and without slowing down leaped through it, landing face down onto the stone floor of the lab. She quickly got up and turned around. Auric's angry, mangled face, illuminated by the fireplace glow, rapidly approached. But he was too late—the darkness in the sphere began solidifying around him. "*No!*" he released a harrowing squeal. "*Not like this. Not like—*"

And then she could hear him no longer. The sphere was solid once again. Auric was trapped in the darkness, alone, surrounded by nothingness. Not a sound, not a sight, not a smell. Absolute nothing, for all of eternity.

"Huzzah!" Percy cried out, holding her to his round belly.

"Au revoir, and good riddance!" Queen Couronne waved, relieved.

"Mijita," Óseo said. "We thought we'd lost yu. ¿How did yu du that?"

She finally allowed herself to breathe. "I figured that if he was right, and I didn't really need my paints to go through the darkness, I could trick him to go in with me, then run away before he could get back out."

Óseo, as well as the rest, was very impressed.

She thought about it some more. The darkness had first allowed her to pass through the back of her closet

without painting. It was her perfect canvas, vast and full of promise.

"I think," she ventured, "maybe we can get to Wherever, after all."

Mrs. Adocchiare looked kindly at her face. "It was always you, dear. It was you whom we were waiting for, in that room," she said.

Queen Couronne rested her hand on Lee's shoulder. "Little princess, Mrs. Adocchiare and I are not headed zere. We still have work to do. I am going back to my kingdoms, and Mrs. Adocchiare is going back to Ze City, oui?"

She understood.

She walked up to the sphere, and stared at it, concentrating hard. The darkness expanded again, then slowly dissolved, revealing the familiar hills where Madame Couronne became Queen.

"À tout à l'heure, mon frères!" she said. She kissed and hugged each of them, warmly—the three friends she had spent centuries in a room with, and the little girl who finally freed her from it.

"Goodbye, Your Majesty." Lee smiled and curtsied. Queen Couronne curtsied back and, holding up the wide flowery bottom of her dress, stepped through the round door onto a hilltop. The sphere fogged up with darkness again, and she was gone.

Mrs. Adocchiare then wobbled over, and at Lee's behest it opened up again, to a brightly illuminated street somewhere in The City.

"I'll miss you," she said, full of sadness.

244

"I'll miss you too, dear." Mrs. Adocchiare pressed her plump finger gently into her dimple. "The footprints of angels." She smiled. "Wasn't I right?"

She smiled back, making her dimples deeper. Mrs. Adocchiare walked onto the street and waved goodbye at them until it was dark again.

It was Óseo's turn next. Even though he was still a skeleton, in her mind he was the young handsome man she shared a dream with. He kneeled down, as he did with his own daughter.

"I… I don't know what tu say, niña."

She shook her head slowly, saying nothing. There was no need. Óseo took her and squeezed her tight in his skeleton arms.

He got up to say his farewells to Percy. Percy reached out his hand for a shake and Óseo grabbed it, pulling him close for a long, warm, brotherly hug.

She focused on Wherever, even though she had no idea where, or even what, exactly, it was. For a long moment, nothing. Then the darkness unfolded once more. Except this time there wasn't a view on the other side. There was only a vast, endless brightness, not blinding but soft, and warm, and absolute. It was the opposite to the darkness. Óseo walked toward the light, and Lee watched as he disappeared in its brilliance.

"It's been a jolly romp, eh?" Percy said, his great white mustache rising with his round cheeks. "But I fear the time has come for me to take my leave as well."

"I know," she said.

"Parting is such sweet sorrow. I shall miss you dearly, Lee. And I shall always cherish our friendship."

She nodded. She tried to keep a brave face, but it crumbled under the weight of her sadness. The four strange people she had found in her closet had become her best friends, and she would miss Percy most of all. "Don't go!" she found herself saying, even though she knew he had to.

"Now, now, child." He took her hands in his. "The bell invites me. I go now in content." He leaned and kissed her forehead tenderly. "It has been a long time for me, my dear. And my darling Felicity must be waiting. Finally… to sleep, perchance to dream…." He smiled at her, a sweet, kind, loving smile, his last smile to her, and walked into the white light. And with that, she was all alone again.

She looked around. The gloomy lab was quiet as a grave, all the humming and buzzing machines laid broken and silent. The orb was opaque black again, floating in the air in front of her, keeping mum. And then the dark sphere rippled, ever so slightly. She stared back, harder, but this time without a place in mind. Not Nowhere nor Elsewhere nor Wherever. Instead, she thought of her father, picturing him in her mind. The darkness stirred. Then it flowed and swirled, until the sphere became a door once again.

ee's mother woke her up, gently. She was sitting on the bed, caressing her hair. She had tears in her eyes.

Lee slowly blinked awake and sat up and realized she was in her own bed. She looked over to the closet; its doors were left open, and she could see the plain white wall at its back. She then caught herself in the mirror on its door—her face and hands and pajamas were covered in smudges of paint.

Ron stood next to her mom, looking baffled at the painting resting on the easel by the bed. It was a portrait of Lee and her father. A very good one. Both of them were laughing.

"Dad's very sorry he never got to say goodbye. He loves both of you very, very much." She looked out the window. The morning sun was coming through the apple trees outside, basking them in golden glow. It was the start of a beautiful day. She couldn't wait for it to be over. She couldn't wait for night to arrive so she could paint again.

ACKNOWLEDGMENTS

What makes an adventure worth going on are the companions you go on it with. I'd like to thank my co-adventurers, starting with my wonderful editor Rebecca Jaycox, who immersed herself in my story as if it were her own and made it better than it could have ever been without her. Also my publisher, Jeffrey Collyer of Aelurus Publishing, a member of a rarely-sighted, endangered species concerned more with what is good and unique than what is sure to sell.

My humble gratitude to the late Neil Gordon, my mentor and friend and the first person who told me I could write that I actually believed, because he didn't have to. My thanks to Joshua Kendall, who guided me through writing my first novel the way a Sherpa guides a novice mountain climber, and to Lorna Owen, who helped me polish a primordial version of this book.

A huge thank-you to Dave Bergman, a true friend, without whose support and conviction this book would never have been finished, let alone published. And to John Chartres, a gentleman and a scholar, who helped me make sure each character's language and cultural nuance are correct.

Most of all, I am grateful to and for my wife Kim, for her guidance (as a bestselling author and editor in her own right) and patience (in changing more than her share of diapers while I shouted out things in different accents in the next room), but above all, for her endless sense of wonder, unfailing optimism, and unwavering goodness. She is my inspiration, every day.

ABOUT

ROY SCHWARTZ

Roy Schwartz has written for newspapers, magazines, websites, academic organizations, tech companies, toy companies, and production studios. *The Darkness in Lee's Closet and the Others Waiting There* is his debut novel.

He lives in Long Island, NY with his wife Kim, their son Ethan, dog Inez, and many, many books, many of which are comic books. When not writing, he is the director of communications of a regional law firm.

Roy can be found at royschwartz.com and on Instagram, Twitter, and Facebook as RealRoySchwartz.

Made in the USA
Middletown, DE
28 May 2021